"I'm Talking About Us."

"There isn't an us," Portia retorted.

"So you keep insisting," Cooper replied. "But I need you to understand something. All that nonsense about men not finding you attractive is just nonsense. You're gorgeous."

Portia smiled. "Thank you. But—"

"I'm not done."

"Oh. Okay."

"But I need you to understand something else. I'm not a nice guy. I'm not selfless. I'm not softhearted."

She was confused by this train of thought. "Oookay."

Well, if she'd been confused before, he was about to make things worse.

He closed the distance between them and pulled her to him. He didn't give her a chance to protest verbally, but pressed his lips to hers. There was a moment of shock. But she didn't resist.

Not even for a second.

* * *

A Bride for the Black Sheep Brother is part of the trilogy At Cain's Command: Three brothers must find their illegitimate sister...or forfeit a fortune.

* * *

If you're on Twitter,
tell us what you think of Harlequin Desire!
#harlequindesire

Dear Reader,

It's always interesting where story ideas come from. About three years ago, I was on a plane when I read an article in the in-flight magazine about skateboarder Tony Hawk and how seamlessly he's transitioned from athlete to businessman. I was fascinated by the fact that this rebellious kid, participating in (what was then) a fringe sport could grow up to be astoundingly successful. Before the flight ended, I ripped the page out of the magazine (sorry, Southwest!) and tucked it away in my bag, determined to one day use that idea for a character.

Flash-forward a year. I was working up the proposal for my At Cain's Command series and knew that my black sheep brother of the Cain family, Cooper Larson, just had to be based (loosely) on Tony Hawk. I switched the sport from skateboarding to snowboarding and went from there.

Flash-forward another few years to this past spring when I was working on this book. Of course, I'd done a little footwork research on Hawk when I was coming up with the idea, but not that much. For the book, I'd focused mostly on snowboarding research. In my personal life, I was doing a whole 'nother set of research. My daughter—who was then seven—was struggling in school. We had decided to test her for dyslexia and ADD, despite the fact that she already qualified for the "gifted and talented" program. When she was feeling anxious about it, I searched famous people with dyslexia and/or ADD on Google. And guess who came up? Tony Hawk.

She and I had great fun reading all about him. Like her, he's smart, talented, driven and sensitive. His parents got him involved in skateboarding so he'd have an outlet for all the energy. Smart parents, too. I guess I should have seen it coming, but now my daughter wants a skateboard. Sorry, honey, but no. Not until you're ten.

Emily McKay

A BRIDE FOR THE BLACK SHEEP BROTHER

EMILY McKAY

ISBN-13: 978-0-373-73322-4

A BRIDE FOR THE BLACK SHEEP BROTHER

This edition published by arrangement with Harlequin Books S.A.

For questions and comments about the quality of this book, please contact us at CustomerService@Harlequin.com.

Printed in U.S.A.

Books by Emily McKay

Harlequin Desire

The Tycoon's Temporary Baby #2097
**All He Ever Wanted* #2188
**All He Really Needs* #2213
**A Bride for the Black Sheep Brother* #2309

Silhouette Desire

Surrogate and Wife #1710
Baby on the Billionaire's Doorstep #1866
Baby Benefits #1902
Tempted into the Tycoon's Trap #1922
In the Tycoon's Debt #1967
Affair with the Rebel Heiress #1990
Winning It All #2031
"His Accidental Fiancée"
The Billionaire's Bridal Bid #2051
Seduced: The Unexpected Virgin #2066

*At Cain's Command

Other titles by this author available in ebook format.

EMILY McKAY

has been reading romance novels since she was eleven years old. Her first Harlequin Romance book came free in a box of Hefty garbage bags. She has been reading and loving romance novels ever since. She lives in Texas with her geeky husband, her two kids and too many pets. Her debut novel, *Baby, Be Mine,* was a RITA® Award finalist for Best First Book and Best Short Contemporary. She was also a 2009 *RT Book Reviews* Career Achievement Award nominee for Series Romance. To learn more, visit her website, www.emilymckay.com.

For my darling daughter, who loves books and reading and stories, despite being bad at "decoding" and being a crappy speller. It's okay, honey. I am, too.

Prologue

Portia Callahan lived her life by one simple rule: when all else failed, make a list.

Today's list was simple, if perhaps a tad more important than most.

- Nails
- Hair
- Makeup
- Dress
- Shoes
- Wedding

Usually, checking items off her list helped her chill out. It soothed her rattled nerves better than a hefty margarita. Not today. Today, she'd checked off the top five items and her insides were still roiling with anxiety. Frankly, she would have ordered the margarita, but a) she was pretty sure smuggling one into the First Houston Baptist Church would put a kibosh on the whole wedding, and b) her hands were shaking so much she was sure she would spill it. If she spilled bright green margarita down the front of the thirty-thousand-dollar gown twenty minutes before the ceremony, her mother's head would actually explode.

A little extreme, maybe, but this was the woman who had taken a nitroglycerin pill this morning when Portia had nearly messed up her manicure.

And that smeared tip on her pinky was nothing compared to her sudden urge to bolt from the church and run down the streets of Houston ripping this white monstrosity off her body. Maybe if her body was moving, her thoughts would stop racing.

Why was her dress so tight? Why was lace so itchy? Why were hairpins so pokey? Had her makeup always felt this sticky?

More to the point, if she felt this panicky now, if she hated the dress and the hairpins and the makeup so much today, when just yesterday they'd all been fine, was it a sign that what she actually hated was the idea of getting married?

Her stomach flipped at the idea. If she didn't do something to calm her nerves, she was going to puke.

But what could she do? Her mother paced along the back of the church's dressing room, critically eyeing every detail of Portia's appearance. Shelby, Portia's maid of honor, stood behind her, doing up the last of the hundred-and-twenty-seven buttons that went up the back of her dress. Portia hated those buttons. Each seemed to cinch her in a little more tightly.

Her body-shaping torture wear constricted her ribs so much she could feel them poking into her lungs. She could barely breathe. And she couldn't help thinking maybe that was the point. Maybe the dress had been designed to squeeze her heart right out of her body.

Just when she thought she couldn't take it anymore, there was a knock on the door.

"Come in," her mother barked.

The door cracked open, and Portia heard the voice of her future mother-in-law, Caro Cain. "Celeste, I don't want to alarm you, but there seems to be a problem with the photographer."

Portia's mother shot her daughter a quick glare. As if this was somehow her mistake, even though she'd personally had nothing to do with the photographer. "Don't move an inch." She looked her up and down. "You look perfect. Just don't mess it up."

And with that, Celeste flounced out of the dressing room to go skewer the hapless person who had created this problem. Portia, meanwhile, sent up a silent prayer of thanks to whatever deity had arranged the snafu.

As soon as her mother left the room, she turned around and grabbed Shelby's hands. "Can you just—?" *Stop trying to strangle me with those buttons!* Portia blew out a breath. Then she smiled serenely. "Could you maybe give me a moment alone?"

Shelby, who had roomed with Portia for all four years at Vassar and knew her better than anyone, frowned and asked, "Are you sure this is a good idea?"

"I'll be fine. I just want a moment to meditate."

"No, I meant—" Shelby gave her hand a squeeze. "Yeah. I'll go keep an eye on your mother. I'll make sure she'd occupied for the next—" She glanced at her watch. "The wedding is in twenty minutes. I can buy you maybe ten minutes alone. That's all."

"Thanks!"

A moment later, Portia was finally, blessedly alone for

the first time in more than nine days. It was almost as good as a margarita. But she felt like every nerve in her body was rubbing against some other nerve and that any second, they might spark and then she'd just—poof—go up in flames.

Her mother had thought the botched manicure was bad. That had nothing on spontaneous combustion.

Alone in the dressing room, she turned slowly in a circle, scanning the room for the distraction she was looking for. Not that there was much room for spinning. Now that she was standing, the acres of white silk that made up the skirt of her dress took up a lot of floor space. She could hardly move in the damn thing. *Huh.* Was that why her mother had insisted on such a monstrously big dress? Had she suspected that Portia might be besieged by last-minute panic and bolt? Had she wanted to guarantee that if Portia did, she'd be easy to take down?

Portia stifled a hysterical giggle at the image of her mother tackling her on the steps of the church.

Not that Portia actually wanted to bolt.

Because she didn't.

This was just nerves. Normal nerves.

Dalton was her match in every way. They were financial and social equals. Which meant that for the first time in life she didn't have to worry about his motives for being with her. She respected him. They got along. And best of all, he was so stable. So steady. And she needed that balance in her life.

They were equals, but opposites. And didn't everyone always say opposites attract?

And she loved him.

Okay, so she was eighty-nine percent sure she loved him. But she was 100 percent sure he loved her. At least, he loved all the parts of her that she showed him. He loved the well-dressed, poised debutante. He loved the best version of her. The person she was trying to be.

And, yes, there was this goofy, rebellious, silly version of Portia, but she was working hard on burying it. Burying it deep. She never went to sing karaoke anymore. She hadn't been skydiving in months. She'd had her Marvin the Martian tattoo removed and the scar was barely visible. Soon, she would be 100 percent the socially acceptable debutante. Soon, she'd be the person Dalton loved.

It wasn't Dalton she wanted to run away from. It was herself.

And the dress. But this was all nerves. She only needed to do something to relieve her tension. Even if it was only for a few minutes. And she knew just what would do the trick.

Coping with the unexpected was one of the things Cooper Larson did best. Zipping down the slopes on his snowboard, he had to be prepared for anything. Everybody knew that snow was mercurial. One second, conditions could appear perfect. The next, it could all go to hell. Cooper's ability to think on his feet and adapt in a spilt second was one of the qualities that had earned him a spot on the Olympic team.

However, both of those skills abandoned him completely when he walked into the bride's dressing room and saw his future sister-in-law standing on her head, her nearly bare legs sticking straight up in the air.

The sight was so unexpected—not to mention confusing—that it took him a while to even figure out what he was seeing. At first all he saw were the legs. It took him a good thirty seconds alone to work his way from the delicate feet down the miles of legs clad only in sheer cream silk, to delicate pale blue garters and eight or so inches of luscious female thigh. And beyond that a pair of bright pink skimpy panties with white dots all over them. Then—just when he thought his head might explode—he realized that the heavy pile of white fluff the legs were sticking out of was an upturned wedding dress.

Shaking his head, he looked again at the legs. Possibly the most fabulous legs he'd ever seen. And they were attached to his future sister-in-law.

Crap.

That was really inconvenient.

What was she doing standing on her head? When she was supposed to be getting married in less than twenty minutes?

And then, he heard her.

"Ba da da da da da!"

Was she singing "Jesse's Girl"?

If that hadn't been Portia's voice, he would have thought he'd wandered into the wrong church. What the hell was going on?

"Portia?" he asked.

The mound of white fluff gave a little squeal. And the legs wobbled precariously. She was going down.

He leaped across the room and grabbed her. Maybe a bit too strongly, because her legs fell against his chest and she kicked him in the face.

"Damn!"

"Ack!"

He stumbled back, dragging her with him.

"Put me down!" she squealed.

But putting her down gently wasn't an easy feat. He took another step back, but then she kicked him again.

"Put me down!" she screamed again.

"I'm trying!"

"Cooper?"

"Yeah. Who else?" Finally, he wrapped an arm around her waist and managed to flip her over. He got a face full of fluffy white lace for his trouble, and her elbow slammed into his chin. He let her go and stepped back, holding his hands out in front of him to ward off her attack. "Are you okay?"

When she looked up, he realized she had a pair of earbuds in her ears and noticed the iPod shoved into the bodice of her dress. She yanked the earbuds out, and he could hear the music playing faintly.

She pushed down her skirt, glaring at him. "Of course, I'm okay. Or rather, I was! Why wouldn't I be okay?"

"You were upside down."

"I was doing a headstand!"

"In your wedding dress?"

She opened her mouth to fire back some quip, but then hesitated, snapped her mouth closed and frowned. "Good point." She grabbed the skirt of her dress and shook it out.

The dress didn't look too bad. Her hair, on the other hand, was a mess. What had obviously once been some kind of fancy twist of curls on the back of her head had started to slide off to the side. One lock of pale golden hair tumbled into her face. Her cheeks were flushed, her lips moist and pink.

He'd known Portia for about two years and in all that time he'd never seen her looking so disheveled. So human. So sexy.

Yeah. And the fact that the image of her bright pink panties and her bare thighs was still seared into his brain had nothing to do with that. And what precisely had been on those panties of hers? From a few feet away, he'd thought they were misshapen white dots, but up close they'd looked like cats. Was that possible? Was there any chance at all that uptight, straitlaced, cold-as-dry-ice Portia Callahan would get married wearing panties with cat heads on them?

"What the hell were you doing?" he asked.

"I was meditating."

"And singing along to eighties pop?"

"I was… I can't…" She blew out a breath that made her hair flutter in front of her face. "It helps me think." And then, she must have realized her hair was mussed, because she grabbed a stray lock of hair and stared at it. "Oh, no! Oh, no, oh, no, oh, no, oh, no!"

She jumped up and ran to the mirror. Still clutching the lock of hair, she turned this way and that, staring at herself in the mirror, muttering "oh, no!" over and over.

He didn't have a lot of experience with panicking women. Zero experience, really. And, to be honest, his mind was still reeling that this was Portia who was panicking. Up until five minutes ago, he would have described her as slightly less emotional than the Tin Man. He would not have pegged her for the type to panic. Or wear pink kitty panties. Damn it, he had to stop thinking about her underwear. And her thighs.

And unless he wanted to be the one to explain to Caro Cain why the wedding was off, he suspected he needed to do some serious damage control.

So he made sure the door was locked and went to stand behind Portia.

He looked at her in the mirror. She was so busy freaking out she didn't notice him until he put his hands on her shoulders. Then she looked up, tears brimming in her dark blue eyes. How had he never before noticed how dark her eyes were? Almost purple, they were so blue.

He dug around in his pocket, but found nothing to give her to wipe her eyes, so he pulled the silk pocket square from his suit pocket and handed it to her.

"Here." She just stared at him, frowning. Crap, he was no good at this. "It's gonna be okay."

"It is?" she asked hopefully.

"Sure."

She stared up at him, a tremulous smile on her lips. "You think so?"

"Yeah." He felt a little catch in his chest. God, he hoped he wasn't lying. "It's just hair, right?" And, that must have been the wrong thing to say, because her lip started wobbling. "I mean, you can totally fix that!" He reached out and gave the lumpy twist a poke. "Just stick in a few more of those pin things, and it'll be fine."

She threw up her hands. "I don't have any more pins!"

"Then how'd you get it up in the first place?"

"I had it done at a salon."

"Oh." He didn't point out that if that was the case, she probably shouldn't have done a headstand. It took a lot of restraint. Surely he got points for that, right? "Well, I bet the ones that came out are still on the ground over there. Let me look." After a minute of crawling around on the floor, he stood up, triumphant. "Five."

She was still sitting in front of the mirror, but she was looking calmer. And she'd done something with her hair so that it looked…more balanced. "Okay. Hand them over."

He did, and then watched as she jabbed them in. When she was done, she met his gaze in the mirror.

"And it's really going to be okay, right?"

"Sure."

"I don't mean the hair."

"Yeah. I got that." He swallowed. Who the hell was he to give relationship advice to anyone? Especially since he couldn't stop thinking about Portia's legs and how adorable she looked in that damn headstand and how she'd always been beautiful but he'd never known how pretty she was until now. “Yeah. It’s going to be okay. Dalton is a good guy. And you’re perfect for each other.”

Except he was lying. Until now, he’d always thought Portia was the perfect girl for Dalton. But this girl? This girl who did headstands in her wedding dress and freaked out and wore pink kitty panties? This girl had more going on inside than he’d ever guessed. This Portia was vibrant and intriguing, and startlingly appealing in this moment of vulnerability. And maybe Dalton wasn’t the right guy for her after all.

One

Twelve years later

Portia Callahan wanted to die of humiliation.

Only one thing kept her from actually doing it. If she died during the Children's Hope Foundation annual gala, the charity's silent auction would bomb. Everyone would be so busy gossiping about how Celeste Callahan had finally berated her daughter to death that no one would raise their paddles to bid.

So instead of dying, Portia stood in the service hallway outside of the Kimball Hotel ballroom and let her mother rant at her.

"Honestly, Portia! What were you thinking?" Celeste's crisp pronunciation grated against Portia's already frayed nerves.

She breathed out a sigh and let go of all the logical, sensible answers she could give. *I was thinking of the chil-*

dren. I was trying to do the right thing. Instead she said what she knew her mother needed to hear. "I guess I wasn't thinking."

Which was also true. Three months ago, when she'd visited the inner-city Houston high school on behalf of Children's Hope Foundation, she hadn't been thinking about how her visit might "look" to the Houston society types. She'd been thinking about connecting with the students, encouraging them to dream of a life beyond minimum wage work. She'd been thinking of them and what they needed. There hadn't even been anyone from the Foundation there that day. It had never occurred to her that the teacher snapping photos might send them in to the Foundation or that a few of them might end up in the photomontage that played in the background at tonight's annual gala. And it had certainly never occurred to her that members of Houston high society might be offended by pictures of her playing a pickup game of basketball with former gang members.

"No, Portia. You clearly weren't thinking. That photo…" Celeste sighed.

God, Portia hated that sound. It was how-could-you-do-this-to-me and what-did-I-do-to-deserve-you all rolled into one exhalation of disappointment.

"It's not that bad," Portia tried to explain. She kept her voice low, painfully aware that they weren't really alone. Sure, her mother had dragged her off into one of the hotel's service hallways, but the gala's waitstaff were filtering past with trays of drinks and appetizers. A couple of them had even slowed down, straining to catch what they could of the argument.

"It would be bad enough if it was just the photo," Celeste said. "But with Laney's pregnancy, everyone is watching you, waiting to see how you'll—"

"Laney's pregnancy?" Portia interrupted. Nausea

bloomed in her stomach, turning those butternut squash appetizers into bricks. "Laney is pregnant?"

Laney was Portia's ex-husband's current wife.

Not that Portia had anything against Laney. Or Dalton for that matter.

She was thrilled, just thrilled, that they'd found love and were blissfully happy. She really was. Or she really tried to be. But it would be easier if her own life didn't feel so stagnant.

And now Laney was pregnant? Portia and Dalton had struggled with infertility for years. But apparently all Dalton needed was a vivacious new wife.

Portia pressed a palm to her belly, willing the appetizers to stay put.

"Laney is pregnant," she repeated stupidly.

"Yes, of course she is. They haven't announced it yet, but everyone has noticed the bump. Honestly, Portia, how do you miss these things? All of Houston has noticed, but you're blissfully unaware of it?"

"I just didn't—"

"Well, you need to. You simply have to be more concerned when gossip is brewing around you. And for God's sake, try not to provide all of Houston with photographic evidence of your midlife crisis."

"It's not a midlife crisis!"

Celeste's gaze snapped from self-pity to anger. "It's a photo of you and five gang members, one of whom is staring down your dress and another of whom has his hand entirely too close to your person."

"He was blocking. He wasn't even touching me!" Was that really how the photo looked to other people? "Mother, it's just a picture. There are fifty pictures in the slide show that illustrate the amazing work the foundation does. One of them happens to have me in it. It's not that big a—"

"It is a big deal," Celeste snapped. "The fact that you think it isn't only shows how naive you are. A woman in your position—"

"My position? What is that supposed to mean?"

"A woman's position in society changes when she goes through a divorce. You've seen this in your own life and in Caro's. Thank God you've fared better than she has. So far."

"Right," Portia said grimly. "Caro."

After her divorce from Dalton, Portia had stayed friends with her former mother-in-law. Caro Cain wasn't the warmest person, but she was still easier to deal with than Portia's own mother. And right now, Caro needed every friend she had. Her divorce from Hollister Cain had left her a social pariah.

"Do you know how many people are out there snickering about that photo?" Celeste demanded.

"Nobody but you cares about that photo!"

Celeste took a step closer. "This is how the world works. Stop being naive."

"It's not naive to want to help children."

"Fine, if you want to help children, I can have Dede set something up."

"I don't need Daddy's press secretary to set up a photo op for me."

"Fine. If you don't want my help, do this on your own. Go make puppets with a kid with cancer, but for God's sake, stay out of the ghetto, because—"

But Celeste never got a chance to finish her thought, because just then, one of the waitresses walked by with a tray of champagne and somehow tripped, spilling a flute of the amber liquid down the sleeve of Celeste's dress.

The older woman reared back, gasping in shock.

The waitress stumbled again and barely stepped out of

the way before Celeste whirled on her. "Why you clumsy, little—"

"Mother, it's okay." Portia grabbed her mother's arm, more out of instinct than out of fear that her mother might hit the girl.

Celeste jerked her arm free, her mouth twisting into a snarl. "I'll have your job for this!"

"Let me handle this, Mother." Portia looked nervously around the hall. It was empty now except for this one waitress. "Go on to the bathroom and clean up what you can. Champagne doesn't stain. It'll be okay."

Celeste just glared at the waitress, who glared back, her jaw jutting out.

Portia guided her mother a step away toward the doorway that led into the ballroom. "I'll handle it. I'll talk to the girl's supervisor."

"That clumsy bitch shouldn't be anywhere near a function like this." Then Celeste flounced off to clean herself up.

Portia turned back to the waitress, half surprised to still see her there. The young woman looked to be in her early twenties. Her hair was dyed a dark maroon, cut short on one side and long on the other. She wore too much eye makeup and had a stud in her nose. And she was glaring belligerently at Portia.

"My name's Ginger, by the way. If you're going to go tattle to my boss."

Portia held up her hand palm out in a gesture of peace. "Look, I'm not going to have you fired, but maybe you could just stay out of Celeste's way for the rest of the night."

Ginger blinked in surprise. "You're not?"

"No. It was an accident."

"Accident. Right." Her tone was completely innocent, but there was a slight smirk to her lips as she stepped toward the door into the ballroom. Her smirk made her look so familiar. “Thanks.”

“Wait a second—” But the door swung open and two more waiters came into the hall and pushed past them. Portia reached for Ginger’s arm and stepped off to the side, where they weren’t in anyone’s way. “Did you do that on purpose?”

“Tip the glass down your mother’s back? Why would I do that?” Ginger smirked again and Portia felt another blast of recognition. Like she should know this girl.

“I don’t know,” Portia admitted. She looked pointedly at the tray of champagne flutes. “But it seems like it’d be awfully hard to tip just one glass without them all spilling.”

“You gonna have me fired or not?”

Portia sighed. “Why would you do that?”

“What? Spill a drink on someone who’s verbally abusing her daughter in public? I can’t imagine why.” Ginger turned as if she was going to stalk off, but stopped and turned back before she reached the door. “Look, it’s none of my business, but you shouldn’t put up with that. Family should treat each other better.”

“Yes. They should.” Portia had no illusions about her mother. She wasn’t sure why she felt as if she had to justify her mother’s words—certainly not to a stranger—but she found herself doing it anyway. “I know my mother can be a bitch. I’m not going to pretend she has my best interests at heart. But when it comes to this kind of thing, she’s almost always right. And I’m usually wrong. If she thinks people will misinterpret those photos of me, then I’d bet money they already have.”

“That’s messed up.” Ginger just shook her head. “That doesn’t bother you?”

“It does, but it’s the world I live in.”

“I don’t care if that’s the world you live in. Family should be on your side. No matter what." Ginger's expression darkened. "The world you live in sucks."

The fierceness in Ginger's gaze took Portia aback for a moment. Portia looked at the girl closely. Again she was struck by how familiar she seemed.

"Have we met before?" she asked impulsively.

Ginger took a step back, the startled movement jostling the champagne flutes on her tray. "No. Where would we have met?"

Before Portia could press her for more information, the waitress spun away and disappeared through the door.

Now Portia was sure they'd met before. It was something in the girl's smile. And something through the eyes.

The eyes.

Portia's breath caught in her chest as the realization hit her.

This young woman. This waitress whom Portia had met by chance had eyes the exact same color as Dalton Cain's. Now that she'd placed the eyes, Ginger's other features seemed to slip right into place. That fierce intensity was pure Griffin Cain. That sarcastic smirk looked just like Cooper's. Ginger was a near perfect amalgamation of the three brothers. Yes, in a more delicate and feminine form, but still, she could be their sister.

Which Portia might be able to dismiss, except for one crucial fact. Dalton, Griffin and Cooper actually had a half sister. They all knew she existed, but no one knew who or where she was. As impossible and unlikely as it seemed, had Portia just found the missing Cain heiress?

Portia looked for Ginger the rest of the night. She constantly scanned the crowd for the waitress's maroon hair and nose stud, but she seemed to have disappeared completely.

By the time Portia had made it back to her small home

at the end of the night, she was determined to track down the waitress. It wasn't that she was obsessed with finding the girl, but it gave her something to think about other than the gossip about her that had been simmering in the background.

Why was it acceptable for people to talk about her merely because her ex-husband was going to be a father? Or because someone had snapped a photo of her playing basketball with some disadvantaged teens? Other people could do truly bad things and no one seemed to care.

The same brutal dynamic was at work with Caro Cain. Hollister Cain, Portia's ex-father-in-law, had had countless affairs. Somehow Caro had held her head up through it all. When Caro divorced him, people gossiped about *her*.

Of course, Hollister and Caro had paid the price for his many affairs. Just last year, when Hollister's health had been so bad, he had received a letter from one of his past conquests. The woman had heard he was on his deathbed and had taunted him with the existence of a daughter he'd never known about.

Whoever had written the letter had known what a manipulative bastard Hollister was. She had known it would drive him crazy to learn he had a daughter he'd never met and couldn't control. When he'd received the letter, Hollister had called his three sons to his bedside—Dalton and Griffin, his legitimate sons, and Cooper, his illegitimate son. He'd demanded that they find the daughter and bring her back into the family fold. Whichever son found her first would be Hollister's sole heir. If she wasn't found before Hollister died, he'd will his entire fortune to the state.

The quest he'd set his sons on had torn the family apart. It had destroyed his own marriage. And now, a year later, the missing heiress still hadn't been found. And Hollister's health had improved. The last time she'd seen him, he'd seemed as bitter and angry as ever, but he was no longer haunted by death. He was just as determined that someone find his daughter.

Maybe it was ridiculous for Portia to think that she might have just found the woman tonight.

As far as she knew, Dalton and Griffin had figured out that their sister was from somewhere in Texas, but that hardly narrowed it down. There were almost thirty million people in Texas.

But of all the people Portia had ever met, only five of them had Cain-blue eyes. Hollister and his sons and now Ginger. This woman with Cooper's smirk and Dalton's determination. She looked just like a Cain.

Not that it was any of her business.

So what if a waitress at a hotel in Houston looked like she could be Dalton's sister?

It didn't have anything to do with Portia.

Except that when Portia thought about Ginger—about the waitress's petulant defiance, about the fierce way she talked about how families should treat each other, Portia felt oddly protective of her. If she was the missing heiress, someone would find her. Someday—maybe someday soon—one of the brothers would stumble on a piece of evidence and they would track her down. Everything about her life would change in a moment. And she was completely unprepared for it.

Ginger was about to be thrust into a world of cutthroat gossips where her every action and motive would be questioned, analyzed and criticized. Where mothers berated their daughters in public and where divorcées were ostracized when they didn't get a lavish divorce settlement.

It was a world of wealth and power, but it was also a crummy world.

But maybe there was something she could do to make this world a little less crummy.

Two

When she was young, Portia had had a reputation among her family for being impulsive, reckless, rash—qualities she had worked hard to banish from her personality in the past fifteen years. And she'd succeeded. No one who knew her now—well, almost no one—would call her reckless.

Now she was not the kind of girl who got a tattoo over summer break—even one of a completely inoffensive, beloved cultural icon like Marvin the Martian. She was not the sort to do headstands in fancy clothes. Those parts of her were gone. It was that simple.

So, a week after the Children's Hope Foundation gala, when she packed her bags and hopped on a plane, it was part of a planned vacation. After all, it was perfectly reasonable for her to take a few weeks of vacation after the months of grueling work on the event. And the Callahans had a condo in Tahoe that she often visited. It wasn't as if she was fleeing from Houston because she couldn't stand the gossip—which hadn't actually been that bad. This was a vacation. A well-thought-out event.

And if she tweaked her travel plans just a smidge so that they included a four-hour layover in Denver, that was totally normal. She'd never liked long flights. Or airports.

And it was also normal—and not at all impulsive—for her to stop by and visit the one person she knew in Denver. Her former brother-in-law, Cooper Larson. Cooper—once the snowboarding darling in the world of extreme sports—was now a successful businessman. He was the CEO and owner of Flight+Risk, which just happened to be headquartered in Denver. He was also possibly the one person who could help her untangle the identity of the Cain heiress.

This was a slight detour in her life. That was all. Visiting Cooper wasn't impulsive or reckless. It was smart. Of the three Cain brothers, he was the least invested in finding Hollister's missing daughter. He had the least at stake. And he was the most likely to know where the young woman was coming from. Visiting Cooper was only logical.

The litany of logical, sensible reasons echoed through her mind as she paid the taxi driver who'd taken her from the airport to Flight+Risk's office in downtown Denver not far from the Sixteenth Street Mall. The building was an older one that had been refurbished. It was sleek and modern inside, while maintaining the sort of informality that suited Cooper's snowboard accessory business. It was exactly what she'd expected of his office. It suited the black sheep of the Cain family.

The only thing that threw her for a loop was Cooper's assistant. She'd expected some young blond snow bunny type. Someone with more style than sense. Someone she could easily talk her way past.

Instead, the woman—Mrs. Lorenzo, according to the

nameplate on her desk—was nearing fifty, with a humorless smile and cold, assessing eyes.

"And what did you say your name was again?"

"Portia Callahan."

"Hmm…" Mrs. Lorenzo looked her up and down, as if Portia might be lying. Then the older woman turned back to the computer, clicked her mouse several times and started typing.

Mrs. Lorenzo must have sensed Portia's doubts, because she raised an eyebrow and made a disapproving *mmm* sound.

"I'm his sister-in-law," Portia threw out hopefully.

Mrs. Lorenzo smirked. "Mr. Larson has one sister-in-law—Laney Cain. She's a lovely young woman. And you are not her."

Portia swallowed, suddenly irritated by this woman's superior attitude. She so didn't need one more person telling her how lovely Laney was. "I'm his former sister-in-law."

"I see." Mrs. Lorenzo's mouth turned down as if Portia had just admitted to being pond scum. "Mr. Larson is in a business meeting out of the office this morning. Would you like to reschedule?"

Portia glanced down at her watch. If she'd done the math right, she had about two hours before she needed to head back to the airport. "No. I'll wait."

"Excellent," Mrs. Lorenzo said grimly. "I'll let him know when he gets in."

With a sigh, Portia picked a chair in the reception area and settled down to wait. She pulled a magazine out of her travel tote and flipped it open, but didn't actually read any of it. Instead, she stared blankly at the brightly colored pictures, her mind racing from the lies she'd been telling herself.

Here was the flaw in her logic: if today's visit to Denver

really was logical and not impulsive, she would not have ambushed Cooper at work, hoping to talk her way past his secretary. She would have called ahead and made an appointment. Or better yet, called him and asked to meet for lunch. Or even better yet, just called and talked through this on the phone.

He was her former brother-in-law. Calling him to chat was perfectly reasonable. She'd talked to him on the phone plenty of times during her marriage to Dalton. And even since the divorce, she'd called a couple of times a year to hit him up for donations to the Children's Hope Foundation.

But instead of just calling, she'd changed her travel plans and come to see him in person. Why?

She looked around the office, felt panic starting to choke her and fought the urge to bolt. What was she doing here? Why had she gone to these drastic lengths? And for a girl she barely knew? Based on nothing more than a pair of blue eyes and a gut feeling?

It was ridiculous. Absurd. Completely irrational.

And that was why she'd come here herself.

Because it was irrational and ridiculous. And she knew if she hadn't jumped in feetfirst, she would have backed out. If she had called and tried to explain this over the phone, she would have panicked and changed her story. She never would have had the guts to actually talk about the missing heiress. She had come here to do it in person because now she was committed. Now, she couldn't back out. She could only wait.

In business, as in snowboarding, talent and preparation only got you so far. After that, it was all a matter of luck. Which sucked, because Cooper Larson had never been a particularly lucky man. Ambitious, yes. Talented, smart and ruthless, yes. Lucky, not so much.

But he was okay with that. Luck was for a privileged few. It wasn't something you could control or work for. And personally, he would much rather owe his success to something he'd done.

Still, when it came to important business meetings, like the Flight+Risk board meeting he had scheduled for the afternoon, he never left anything to chance. The meeting would be held at a hotel conference room, not far from Flight+Risk's headquarters. He'd spent the morning at the hotel, putting the finishing touches on the proposal he'd be bringing before the board. Which left him just enough time to stop back by the office and check in before grabbing lunch and heading to the board meeting.

Except Portia was waiting to see him when he got there.

For a moment, he just stopped cold in the doorway staring at her. "Portia?" he asked stupidly. "What are you doing here?"

She stood up, looking strangely nervous. "I had a layover in Denver. And I thought maybe we could talk."

She'd been reading a magazine when he walked in and now she rolled it tightly in her hands, clenching it as if maybe she wanted to swat the nose of some naughty dog.

He studied her, taking in the white of her clenched knuckles. The faint lines of strain around her eyes. He hadn't seen her often since her divorce from Dalton—hell, he hadn't seen her often during their marriage—but he knew her well enough to recognize the signs of stress and nerves.

Even though it would mess with his schedule for the day, he nodded toward his office. "Sure. Come on in." He glanced toward his secretary with a nod. "Hold my calls."

Mrs. Lorenzo narrowed her gaze infinitesimally in disapproval. "Sir, shall I send you a reminder, oh, say thirty minutes before your meeting?"

Good ol' Mrs. Lorenzo could always be counted on to impose a rigid schedule. He grinned. "Make it twenty minutes."

If he skipped lunch that would leave plenty of time to walk back over to the hotel.

He led Portia into the office and gestured toward one of the chairs, admiring the subtle sway of her hips as she preceded him. Portia was built exactly the way he liked—tall and lean. Today she wore her pale blond hair back in a sleek ponytail. She was dressed in skin-tight jeans and a white shirt under a tan sweater. Everything about her looked cool and confident. Everything except those white knuckles.

Though he gestured her toward a chair, he didn't sit behind his desk. Instead, he propped his hips on the desktop and stretched his legs out in front of him. Frankly, he hated the trapped feeling that came with sitting behind a desk for too long. It reminded him of school. And with the board meeting this afternoon, he was going to spend enough time sitting still.

"What's up?" he asked as soon as Portia sat down.

She bobbed back to her feet before answering. "I think I've found the heiress."

"Who?" he asked.

"The missing Cain heiress. The one Dalton and Griffin have been searching for so frantically. Your sister. I've found her."

"What?" He frowned. Her answer was so unexpected, so completely out of left field, his brain spun. No, not even left field. Out of no field. "I didn't even know you were looking for her."

"I wasn't!" Portia started pacing, her words pouring out of her. "I was at a fund-raiser. The big Children's Hope Foundation gala. And I just met this girl. She's about the right age, mid-twenties. Her hair's red, but I'm pretty sure it was dyed. But she has the Cain eyes."

He rolled his own eyes at that, but he was surprised by the way those words drove the tension right out of his body. "The Cain eyes? That's what you're basing this on? The fact that she has blue eyes?"

Portia paused on the far side of his office, right in front of the wall of books he'd never read that the decorator had picked out. He got the feeling that Portia wasn't studying the book spines, but rather summoning her courage before turning back to look at him. She jutted out her jaw as she frowned. "It's a real thing. Don't act like it isn't."

"I'm not acting. Ten percent of the population have blue eyes. They can't all be related to the Cains. Not even Hollister slept around that much."

She blew out a frustrated breath. "Listen, there are some things women are better at than men. Facial recognition—including eye color—is one of them." He waggled his hand in a that's iffy gesture. "Trust me on this. Cain-blue eyes are very unique. I spent ten years staring into Dalton's eyes. I know that color. And I've never seen anyone else with those eyes except for Hollister and his sons. This girl—this girl I saw at the fund-raiser—she's your sister. That has to mean something to you."

Cooper shifted and studied Portia.

She was such a mystery. Half the time, she came off as this coolly serene princess. No, more than half. Eighty percent, maybe ninety percent of the time. But he'd seen another side of her. He knew she had more going on than the ice princess thing most people saw. He couldn't forget when he'd walked in on her doing a headstand on her wedding day. Every time he saw her he thought of those long legs and the pink kitty cat underwear. A guy never forgot a thing like that. He never forgot the sharp punch of desire. Even when the woman had spent a decade married to his brother.

But Portia wasn't married to Dalton anymore. She was here in his office. A thousand miles from her home. Talking to him about something she easily could have told Dalton.

What was up with that?

He ran his thumb along his jaw. "Okay. So let's say this is the girl. Let's say she's really the heiress. Why come to me? Why not just call up Dalton?" And then it hit him—of course she wouldn't call Dalton. He was her ex-husband. Yeah, their divorce seemed civil enough. From the outside. But who knew what it had been like from her side of things? Just because she'd kept in contact with Caro and Hollister that didn't mean she wanted Dalton to win the challenge so that he could inherit all of Cain Enterprises. "Never mind. Sorry I said that. That was stupid. Of course you're not just going to hand him the money. But why not talk to Griffin about this?"

She pulled a sheepish face. "I'm not exactly Griffin's favorite person. I don't know if he'd even believe me. But in reality I couldn't go to him for the same reason I couldn't go to Dalton."

"The same reason? Jesus, how many of us have you married?"

She narrowed her gaze, looking confused for a second before shaking her head. "Very funny. Yeah, sure, I'm not Dalton's biggest fan right now, but that's not what I meant."

"What did you mean?"

"I couldn't talk to Dalton because he wants it too badly," she said simply, like he was the idiot for not seeing it right off.

"You can't tell him you think you've found the girl because he wants to find her?" he asked slowly, drawing the words out while he tried to wrap his brain around what she meant.

"Yes! Think about it—if the girl isn't found before something happens to Hollister, then Cain Enterprises is going to be in serious trouble. If Hollister's shares of the company go to the state, they'll probably be auctioned off, most likely to Cain's competitors. The company will be in ruins. Even though Dalton doesn't work for Cain Enterprises anymore, he doesn't want that to happen. He's worked his ass off for Cain all his life. A new job doesn't change that. He still loves the company. He's always going to pick what's best for Cain Enterprises. He's not going to think twice about his sister."

"So you're telling me you haven't gone to Dalton with this information because you're worried about the heiress?"

"Exactly. Someone needs to think about what's best for this poor girl."

Cooper raised an eyebrow. "This poor girl? If you're right, this poor girl is worth hundreds of millions of dollars. Probably more money than she's ever dreamed of. No one would call this girl *poor.*"

Portia seemed to hesitate, then smiled faintly. "Perhaps *poor* isn't quite the word I meant, but I'm sure you'll agree, if Dalton and Griffin do find her, she's going to have a rough time of it."

"What's that supposed to mean?"

"Just that the Cains live in a world of wealth and power that most people can't even imagine. You and I both know that if you're unprepared for that world, it will gobble you and devour you whole. This girl, she didn't grow up with money."

"How exactly do you know she's poor?" he asked with a bit of a sneer. "Are you guessing based merely on the way she was dressed or is this something she told you while you were gazing into her Cain-blue eyes?"

"Very funny. But trust me, I know. She's a waitress, with dyed red hair and one of those little studs in her nose."

"You think rich kids don't rebel? Because I've got to tell you, I've made a lot of money in an industry that's all about rich kids rebelling."

"Exactly. When rich kids rebel, they go snowboarding in Utah. Kids working jobs as waitresses at a hotel? Those kids don't have time to rebel."

Well, she had a point there. And he might even be willing to help her; her heart was in the right place, even if it wasn't really her business anymore. After all, he'd always liked Portia—hell, he'd always more than liked Portia. That was part of the problem, though, wasn't it? It wasn't appropriate to more-than-like your sister-in-law. Not that she was his sister-in-law anymore. Was there some sort of statute of limitations on that?

But he was getting off track. Regardless of how he felt about Portia, it was hard to be too enthusiastic about helping out when her entire reason for asking for his help was because he didn't fit into her world.

"I can't tell Dalton where to find her," Portia said. "He wouldn't think twice about thrusting her into this completely unprepared. And I'm not saying that because I think he's jerk. He just wouldn't even think. He always put business first. He wouldn't hesitate."

"And you think I would?"

"Hesitate?" She shrugged. "I think you know better than anyone where this girl is coming from. She has a middle-class background at best. She won't know what she's getting into. She'll be vulnerable and unprepared—"

"Yeah. I get it." Cooper cut Portia off with a sharp wave of his hand. Jesus, was this how people had seen him when he'd first gone to live with the Cains? "It's probably not as bad as you think. I'm sure she'll at least be potty trained."

"That's not what I meant." Portia glared at him, but she looked more exasperated than angry. "I'm trying to protect her."

"Fine. So mentor her or whatever. Take her under your wing. This doesn't have anything to do with me."

"If I'm right and she really is Hollister's daughter, then she's your sister. It has everything to do with you." She tilted her head just a little and eyed him. "Besides, you can't tell me that you aren't at least a little bit interested in winning. In doing what neither Dalton nor Griffin has been able to do. It's a lot of money."

An ugly thread of disgust wound through his stomach. He got so damn sick of these games people played. If asking didn't get what you want, why not manipulate and pit people against one another? That's exactly what Hollister had been doing for years.

Cooper pushed himself to feet. "I don't give a damn about Hollister's money. I never have. If I had, then I'd been one of Cain Enterprises' lackeys right now instead owning my own company."

"Fine. You don't want the money? Give the money away. Give the money to me."

"You don't need the money any more than I do."

"Please, Cooper—"

"Why?" he demanded. "Why on earth do you care so much about this girl?"

She bumped up her chin again. "Because family is supposed to take care of each other, that's why."

"You're not part of the family anymore."

She went instantly still, and for a second, he would have sworn she'd even stopped breathing. Damn it. It was as if his words had skewered her.

Then resolve settled in her gaze. "You're right. I'm not part of this family anymore. But I was for ten years and I know how hard the Cains can be. I had to fight tooth and nail to get Caro to accept me and treat me with respect. I never won over Hollister, and I'm embarrassed to say I stopped trying long after I should have. He is a hard man. Brutal. And even though I love Caro like she's my own mother, I would be very surprised if she welcomes this girl with open arms. And why should she after the way Hollister treated her in the divorce?" She blew out a breath then, and he could tell she had to work to make it sound even. To make it sound like she wasn't already emotionally invested. "This girl is your family. Don't you want to help her?"

Did he want to help this girl? This stranger who might be his sister? Hell, he didn't know.

Cain family politics didn't interest him. At all.

He didn't give a damn about what happened to the company or to Hollister. None of this was his problem. And frankly, he didn't buy half of what Portia was telling him.

He leveled his gaze at her. "Okay, enough with the warm-fuzzy garbage. What aren't you telling me?"

She pulled back and blinked rapidly. "I don't know what you're talking about."

"Come on, you came here in person to beg me to do this and you expect me to believe your only motive is family loyalty to a girl you spent five minutes with?"

He half expected her to have some visible reaction, but Portia was a cool one, and even though he knew he'd hit on something, she didn't so much as flinch. But he could see the calculations going on behind her eyes, so he didn't trust her words when she calmly said, "Fine. You want a motive? How does this one work? I know you don't want the money, so I'm hoping you'll give it to me."

For a second, all he could do was stare at her. There

was a hard glint in her eyes, a stubborn tilt to her chin, that almost—almost—made her statement believable. But not quite.

"All right," he said, wanting to see where she was going with this.

Her chin bumped up a little. "I…um…the divorce left me destitute. I need the money."

"You're destitute?"

"Totally broke."

"Nice try. I don't believe you're broke. Not for a minute."

She frowned, scrunching her mouth to the side adorably. "Really."

"No. When you and Dalton got married, Hollister told me you had a trust from your paternal grandparents that was worth over fifteen million. I know Dalton didn't touch it. So unless you expect me to believe that you've blown through fifteen million in two years…"

She sighed. "I could be really bad with money?"

"No." He didn't believe that, either. He cocked his head to the side. "But I do believe you want the money. Why?"

She frowned again, and he sensed that she was trying to decide exactly what to tell him. Finally, she said, "Have you talked to Caro lately?"

"Caro?" he asked, surprised by the sudden change in topic. "No. Why?"

"Because things haven't gone well for her since the divorce. Personally. Socially. Financially. And I just thought… if you really don't want the money, then we could give some of it to her."

"She needs money?" But then he waved aside his own question. "Of course she needs money. Hollister's such a bastard, he probably butchered her in the divorce. Jesus. Do Dalton and Griffin know?"

"I don't think anyone knows. She and I haven't always

been close, but we are now. I see it, but she doesn't even admit it to me. Besides, she's not exactly their favorite person right now."

"Yeah. I guess not," he agreed. The mysterious letter about Hollister's missing daughter had turned their lives upside down. Neither Dalton nor Griffin had been particularly thrilled to find out that the letter hadn't been penned by some anonymous former lover of Hollister's, but by his angry and bitter wife. "So Hollister eviscerated her in court and she's too proud to tell her sons that she needs financial help. But you think she'll take money from me?"

"I know she's probably not your favorite person, either—"

"I have no problem with Caro," he said quickly. "I never have."

"Oh," Portia said softly. "I just assumed."

It was a fair assumption. Caro was easy to characterize as his wicked stepmother. But that didn't mean they were enemies or that he wanted her out on the street.

"Caro and I get along fine," he said. "But I don't think she'd take money from me."

"She might if it was Hollister's money. He screwed her over. I think she'd enjoy screwing him back." Portia's face settled into resolve. "I could convince her."

Which brought him back to square one: he didn't have time for this.

"Look, it's not about whether or not I want to help her. I don't have the time. It's not my problem."

"But Caro—"

"Look, I can find a way to help Caro without finding this missing heiress." And he would find a way to help her. Just not now. He glanced down at his watch. "And I've got a meeting I'm going to be late for. I'm sorry, Portia."

He took one last look at Portia. She was perfect and pristine and untouchable. God, sometimes she was so pretty, it almost hurt to look at her. And other times, her beauty seemed almost too fragile. Like she might shatter. He was never sure if the part that would shatter was the real woman or only the outer shell that she showed the world.

In the decade she'd been married to his brother, he'd stayed far away from her because it had been the right thing to do. Now that she was single, he had other reasons for staying away. They weren't from the same world. He'd learned as a kid what it meant to be an outsider in that world. What it meant to be Hollister Cain's bastard son. Seeing the things other people had. Reaching for them. Having your hand slapped away.

Yeah. He knew what it meant to want things you couldn't have.

And yeah, he knew that this mystery sister—whoever she ended up being—was going to have a hell of a time adjusting. But he also knew that nothing he did was going to make it any easier on her. She'd either be strong enough or she wouldn't. She'd have to find her own way. Just like he had.

"She has your smile," Portia said. "If that matters at all."

His step faltered only a little. "If she has you on her side, she'll be just fine."

With that, he left the office, putting the conversation and everything it had stirred up behind him. His future rested on the outcome of the board meeting he was going to. He didn't need this Cain family drama. He didn't need a sister. And he sure as hell didn't need Portia here tempting him.

Three

Three hours later, Cooper sat at the head of the conference table and watched his dreams spiral down the drain.

The board voted no.

By a wide margin. It wasn't even close.

Nine of the twelve board members had voted against his plan to get Flight+Risk into the hotel business. Millions could be made in an upscale resort catering specifically to snowboarders. His gut had told him this was a solid venture. But apparently the board thought his gut was "fiscally irresponsible at this juncture."

Now, as the board members started to filter out of the hotel conference room—the votes cast, the meeting officially adjourned—they could hardly meet his gaze. Which was fine, since he feared he might lunge across the table and slam his fist into Robertson's face. The bastard had been on the board since the company's inception. The man—a staid, lifelong businessman in his sixties—had a background in the retail industry that had proved invaluable, but he had little to no imagination. If you couldn't sell it at Macy's, he wasn't interested. He'd been an opponent of Cooper's resort plan from the beginning, but Cooper had really thought he'd won over enough of the other board members. Clearly, he'd been wrong.

With the exception of a couple stragglers, the room cleared within two minutes. An obvious sign that the board wasn't any more comfortable with the outcome than he was. They may have voted against him, but no one wanted to face him down. As for the part of him that wanted to beat the crap out of someone as a result? Well, that was a part that he'd worked hard to bury beneath the facade of a successful businessman.

So he'd waited quietly for the board to leave. He just sat there at the head of the table, staring blankly at the stack of pages in front of him while the rats fled the sinking ship. When he looked up, only two other people remained—Drew Davis, the only fellow snowboarder on the board, and Matt Ballard, the Chief Technology Officer of FJM, a green energy company out of the Bay Area, and a good friend of Cooper's.

After a moment of silence, Drew said, "Man, you're so screwed."

"I'm not screwed." But Cooper said it grimly and with no real conviction.

"No, you're totally f—"

"No. I'll convince them."

There was too much at stake in this fight. This was *his* company. Flight+Risk made the best, toughest gear for winter sports. The best snowboards, the best jackets, the best thermals. All of it. He knew it was the best for two reasons: first off, because he'd designed most of it himself and demanded absolute perfection. Second, because every top snowboarder in the world wanted to use his gear. Yes, it was that good. He made sure of it himself, because inferior gear put people's lives at risk. And profits as well, though that had always been a secondary consideration for him. Still, his perfectionism, ambition and determination had made him a legend on the half-pipe and in the business world.

So why the hell didn't his board trust that he was right about this?

"How exactly are you going to convince them?" Matt asked, rocking back in his chair. Matt had pulled his laptop out the second the meeting was over and was typing now. He was one of those unique guys who could manage to do multiple things at once. Probably because he was freakin' brilliant. He'd been Flight+Risk's first private investor. In fact, he'd approached Cooper as a fan and offered him start-up money before the company had been more than a business plan and prototype board. They'd become good friends over the years.

Somehow it didn't make Cooper feel any better that the only two members of the board who voted yes with him were his two best friends. It smacked of pity votes.

He looked first at Drew and then at Matt. "You can't honestly tell me you agree with Robertson that investing in another manufacturing facility is a better use of our money?"

"Not better," Drew said. "Less risky."

"My plan isn't risky," Cooper said stubbornly.

"You want to invest forty million dollars in this," Drew said. "Flight+Risk will be overextended. Of course the board is going to balk."

"The company has stellar credit and it will only be for the next eighteen months. The location I've picked is perfect. There's already a resort there—"

"A dated, crummy hotel," Matt interjected.

"And, yes, it needs renovations, but the preliminary inspector said the building was sound." The hotel he'd found, Beck's Lodge, was aging and currently unprofitable, but he knew he could turn it into something amazing. "The snow out there is perfect. As soon as the resort opens, the returns on this investment will be huge. You know I'm right."

"Yeah," Drew said. "I think you're right. But the board cares more about what the stock market thinks."

"Being overextended isn't the problem," Matt said without looking up.

Drew and Cooper both turned to look at Matt.

"What?" Drew asked.

"Then what is the problem?" Cooper asked.

"It's a problem of perception." Matt looked up as if surprised to be the center of the attention. "Come on. Cooper has a reputation for taking crazy risks. That incident with the model after the Olympics when you were reprimanded is a perfect example. And everyone knows Flight+Risk nearly failed in the first two years and would have if you hadn't been pumping your own money into the company to keep it afloat."

"You're saying the board didn't vote against the idea. They voted against me."

"The media loves that stuff," Matt said, shrugging. "It makes for great reading. But the kinds of risks you take scare the hell out of investors."

"Those kinds of risks pay off."

"Barely."

"No. Every one of the risks I've taken in business has paid off huge."

"Yes. They did pay off huge. After you almost failed miserably. You've had a lot of success, but your winning streak is going to end someday. No one wants to catch the flak from that."

"So you're saying everyone just thinks it's my time to fail."

"Yeah."

"But this isn't risky. By the time I'm done with this resort, the best snowboarders in the world will be there. If I were a golfer building one of those golf communities, everyone would be clamoring to invest."

"Maybe." Matt shrugged and looked back down at his laptop. "But golf is different. Those guys know rich. You're just a snowboarder."

Just a snowboarder?

That pissed him off. Yeah, he knew Matt didn't mean it personally, but it was hard not to take it that way.

Because even if Matt didn't buy that argument, plenty of other people did. Never mind that Cooper had been running Flight+Risk for three times as long as he'd been a professional snowboarder. He had more money now than any one man could spend in a lifetime and had earned his money himself, unlike so many other rich bastards. And he'd never once made a business decision that hadn't paid off. Never mind any of that.

In the end, the board was scared he didn't have the business chops to know a great investment from a pipe dream. They'd pegged him as too much of a risk taker just because he'd left college to snowboard professionally. They thought he didn't know the upscale market just because he'd had to work for every one of his successes. Because he'd worked hard to keep his relationship to the Cains on the down low. He'd never wanted people handing him things because of who his father was. He'd never wanted the Cain name to buy him anything. So sure, his lineage was out there for whoever dug around in his past—and reporters loved that nonsense—but he didn't advertise it. He'd never taken the Cain name, even though he'd lived with Hollister and Caro after his mother had died. He never talked about his father or his family connections.

He would have laughed at the irony if it hadn't pissed him off so damn much.

Would he have to put up with this kind of thing if he'd been in the habit of reminding the board who his father was? If he'd trotted out his father's name, the board probably would have rolled right over.

Instead, he did things his own way and his ideas were labeled too risky.

It wasn't fair.

Which was fine. His life had never been fair. He was the king of making not-fair work for him.

He looked up suddenly to realize that his two friends were exchanging worried glances. As if he'd been quiet too long and they were concerned he was plotting Robertson's demise. Well, he was, but not in the way they were worried about.

So he smiled broadly and stood. "It's all good."

Drew stood also. "Are you okay?"

"Yeah. It's just time for Plan B."

Matt raised his eyebrows. "Really? 'Cause I heard you say once that backup plans were for losers without the determination to get it right the first time."

Yeah. That sounded like him. He shrugged. "Okay, we'll call this Plan 2.0."

Matt snapped his laptop closed and stood. "So what's Plan 2.0?"

"I'm going to convince the board that this isn't risky. I'm going to convince them that I do know this market."

"They've already voted you down. Flight+Risk can't move forward unless it comes to a vote again," Matt pointed out.

"I got too eager and pushed the vote too soon. But by

the time I'm done with them, they'll be desperate to get Flight+Risk involved."

"How exactly are you going to do that?" Drew asked.

"I'm going to hire an expert."

In the end, Portia missed her flight to Tahoe and had to reschedule for the next day. The airline had pulled her suitcase off the flight and had held it in Denver, thank goodness, and she'd been able to find a car service to deliver her bag to her hotel. It was all far less inconvenient than it might have been. No matter how Portia tried to tell herself that she'd only lost one day and that she hadn't gone that far out of her way, she couldn't help feeling that the entire trip had been a huge waste of time.

For tonight, she'd checked into a hotel in Denver, not far from Flight+Risk's corporate offices. In the morning she would see about getting another flight to Tahoe. But now, she had room service coming with a salted caramel brownie and carafe of red wine.

Yes, tomorrow she would start her vacation. She'd still get her two weeks of solitude at her parents' summer cabin by the lake. She'd read the dozen or so books already loaded onto her Nook. She'd watch movies. Do some yoga. It would all be very relaxing.

Except she wasn't relaxed. Her mind was still whirling with thoughts of the waitress from the Kimball Hotel, the woman she knew was Hollister's daughter.

Part of her agreed with Cooper. She should just let it go. It wasn't any of her business.

Honestly, she hadn't given the Cain heiress much thought in the year since Hollister had issued the challenge. However, now that she'd met the woman, she couldn't stop worrying about her. She knew better than anyone what a brutal man Hollister was. He was no one's ideal father-in-law. He'd criticized her endlessly. He'd only gotten worse once her fertility problems became public knowledge.

Dalton hadn't put up with that, of course. He'd called his father on it every time he'd witnessed it. But Dalton hadn't been around much. Caro had stepped up to her defense, as well. That was how she and Caro had gotten so close. At first, Hollister's behavior had hurt. She hadn't realized he treated everyone badly. He wasn't picking on her. He was just a jerk.

Would Ginger know that?

She'd seemed tough. Would she be able to defend herself against the likes of Hollister? Would she understand that any sign of weakness would stir up the piranhas? Would she have any defenses against the people who would pretend to be her friend and then turn on her in a second?

Yes, Cooper was right. It wasn't Portia's business. But that didn't stop her from worrying about the girl. She'd been counting on Cooper to take over finding the heiress for her. The hope that some of his reward money would be funneled to Caro was just the salted caramel topping on the brownie. Now that he'd refused, she was left in the hot seat again. She had no other ideas about how to help Caro or the heiress. Unless she went to Dalton.

Still, she couldn't shake the feeling that being found was going to change this woman's life forever, and not necessarily in a good way. But what could she do? Not telling anyone that she'd found the heiress wasn't an option. Damn Cooper for not agreeing to help her. Really, she'd thought better of him.

A moment later there was a knock on the door. Men may never do precisely what she expected them to do, but thank goodness for chocolate. It was there when she needed it.

But when she opened the door, it wasn't room service with her brownie. It was Cooper.

He leaned casually against the wall right outside her hotel room, one ankle crossed over the other. He was wearing the same suit he'd had on earlier in the day, but the tie was gone and the jacket looked rumpled. Like he'd taken it off several times over the past few hours.

He looked up when she opened the door. "Hey, I need a favor."

"You're not a brownie," she muttered under her breath.

He blinked, looking surprised. Then his mouth curled in a wry smile. "Not the last time I checked."

"I ordered a brownie from room service." God, that sounded pathetic. A woman eating a brownie alone in a hotel room? It practically screamed *loser*. "It has a salted caramel topping."

Nope. That didn't sound any less pathetic.

Thank God, she hadn't mentioned the carafe of red wine.

He had texted her over two hours earlier saying he wanted to stop by to talk, so she'd sent him her room number, but when he never showed up, she'd assumed he'd decided against it.

Cooper ignored her babbling and asked, "Can I come in?"

Tempted though she was to demand he go find her brownie as a gesture of goodwill, she stepped aside and let him enter.

He walked into the room and shut the door behind him. Her hotel was one that catered to businesspeople, so her room was a minisuite, with a small living area and kitchen. Before the knock, she'd been about to settle onto the sofa and watch a movie she'd bought on pay-per-view. A sappy romantic drama she'd already seen. The title of the movie was splashed across the screen in pause mode. She clicked the TV off, feeling strangely ashamed of her choice. Next time she was picking an action movie. Or one of those comedies with all the frat-boy humor.

She glanced back over to see Cooper studying her. "What?" she asked self-consciously.

"Nothing." His full lips curved into a smile. "I don't think I've ever seen you looking..." His words trailed off like he didn't have the faintest idea how to describe her appearance.

She glanced down. Her yoga pants and hoodie were about the least glamorous things she owned. "I'm not going to apologize for not being better dressed. It's late. You came to me. You're the one who texted and said you want to talk."

"I'm not criticizing. It's adorable."

There was a gleam of amusement in his gaze. Amusement and something else, as well. Something that made her belly flutter around a bit.

God, he was good-looking. Attractive in a way that completely disarmed her. There was no polish to him. He had no smooth edges. He was rugged and rough-hewn, like the harsh landscapes he snowboarded. But there was an innate humor to him also. A lightness—the way the sun could still shine on a bitterly cold day on the slopes.

Not many men she knew managed to pull that off—his unique combination of tough and disarming. But he did. He wielded his charisma like a surgeon's knife, and if she wasn't careful, he'd lure her in and slice away at her defenses.

She rolled her eyes. "Stop trying to charm me. Just tell me what you want so I can eat my brownie in peace."

"You don't have your brownie yet," he pointed out.

"Exactly. Which gives you from now until whenever the brownie arrives to convince me not to kick you out."

"Then I better talk fast."

And he did. Fast and passionately. She clocked him.

For two straight minutes he talked about his plan to buy and renovate some resort in Southern Utah. He waxed poetic about the perfect powder and the lack of true luxury hotels in the area. He talked about the untapped market. Thirty seconds in, she sank to the sofa and tucked her legs up under her, exhausted just watching him pace the tiny length of the room. He was still talking when there was a knock on the door.

She stood and gestured toward the door. "My brow—"

He stopped right in front of her and grabbed her arm. "Wait. I'm not done."

"But my—"

"You said I had until the brownie arrived." He grinned. "It's not in the room, yet. Give me thirty more seconds."

Cooper on a full tear was an impressive thing. "Look, I'm sorry your board didn't agree. I think it sounds like a great idea. But I don't see what this has to do with me."

"Maybe the board is right. Maybe I don't know that high-end luxury market well enough. I'm just a kid from Denver who happens to be good on a snowboard. But you do know that market. I want you to visit the hotel. See if you agree that it can be turned into a playground for the rich."

"I don't know anything about the hotel business."

"I don't, either. I'm not asking you to run the hotel. I just want your opinion. You grew up with money and—"

"Cooper, *you* grew up with money," she protested.

"No. I grew up with money during the summers. For two miserable years I lived with the Cains in high school. That's not the same and you know it. I never fit in. You said yourself that I was the perfect person to find the Cain heiress because I know what it's like to be an outsider. But you were born to this life. And you have the best taste of anyone I've ever met. And—"

There was another knock on the door and he held out his hand as if to stall for more time.

"Do you really think keeping me from my brownie is going to help your argument?"

A few minutes later, after the waiter had come and gone, she turned back to find Cooper watching her with a mischievous gleam in his eyes. Maybe getting that brownie hadn't been a good idea. Clearly, it had bought him just enough time to concoct some scheme.

"If you help me convince the board to buy Beck's Lodge, then I'll help you find my sister. I'll clear a whole week from my calendar to help her get settled. No, a whole month." He raised his eyebrows. "What do you think?"

"I help you, you'll help me?"

"Exactly."

Her heart rate ticked up a notch. Wasn't that what she wanted? His help with the heiress?

But helping him would mean staying here—or wherever this lodge of his was—at least for a few more days. Maybe more. It would mean spending a lot of time in Cooper's company. For some reason that thought made her deeply uncomfortable. He was an undeniably attractive man. She'd have to be dead not to notice that. Not that she thought of him that way, but it did make this entire situation more confusing.

She gazed longingly at the room service tray and her brownie. Right about now, she could certainly use the comfort only a bakery item could provide. Just a few minutes alone with her brownie. Was that really too much to ask?

"So are you in?" Cooper asked.

"Is there any chance you're going to let me off the hook here?"

"Very little."

So, apparently, yes. It was too much to ask.

"What do you think?" he asked.

"I think you're crazy. That's what I think. You took too many blows to the head on the half-pipe."

"But you'll do it?"

"I didn't say that." His smile brightened as if she'd just given in. "And no. I won't."

His smile deepened. "Yeah. You're going to do it."

"I just said I wasn't going to."

"Yeah. I noticed that. But you'll change your mind."

"I won't," she said, not because she really believed it but because…well, no one liked feeling that transparent.

"You will. You'll do it because you're desperate. You traveled all the way here to talk to me into this. That's how much you want this."

"I'm not desperate!" she protested.

He ignored her. "That's the problem with wanting things too badly. It puts you at a disadvantage when it comes to negotiating." His grin widened, making her breath catch in her chest. "Next time you want something from me, you should play it a little cooler. Maybe call before you rush all the way here."

Damn him for seeing through her so completely. Damn him for calling out her weaknesses. And damn him for making her like him despite those two things.

She crossed her arms over her chest and blew out a breath. "I'll try to remember that in the future."

Four

Twenty minutes later, Portia was washing down the last bite of her brownie with a healthy sip of red wine. She'd shared the brownie with him. He'd eaten his half in three bites; she had carefully divided hers into tiny cubes and eaten it with her fork. Cooper loved the way she turned eating a brownie into an art.

"What do you think?" he asked.

She paused, fork in her mouth, and then studied him through narrowed eyes as she slowly pulled the fork out. "What you really need to do is bring the board out to this hotel. Show them its potential firsthand."

"The place is a wreck right now," he admitted. "I don't think they'll get past that."

"So you make it look like it isn't a wreck. You feed them good food and drinks. You distract them."

"You want me to throw a party to convince them?"

"I'm thinking more a snowboarding exhibition, proceeded by a party."

"So you'll do it?"

"I'm still mulling."

"You can't mull any faster?"

"Not all of us think as fast as you do. Besides—" she glanced at her wrist where a watch would be if she was wearing one "—it's after eight on Monday night. There's a whole twelve hours before you could do anything even if I agree. And you're the one who told me not to appear too desperate."

She leaned forward and carefully set the fork across her plate before putting the silver dome back over it and nudging the room service tray across the coffee table. There was grace in her every movement. She was a woman made for room service and luxury hotels. Elegance practically seeped from her pores. Beside her he felt like a buffoon.

Watching her eat a brownie—a simple brownie for God's sake—reminded him of the thousand and one ways she outclassed him. He was used to feeling outclassed. That's how he'd spent every summer of his youth. He just wasn't used to wanting the kind of woman who made him feel that way.

"I don't think I'm the right woman for you," Portia said, her tone almost distracted.

"What?" He sat up a little straighter.

She frowned, confused for a second, then blushed. "I meant I don't think I'm the right woman for this job. You should hire a professional party planner. Or possibly an independent consultant. Maybe both."

"That's why I'm hiring you. You can do the job of both. I know how flexible you are."

Her gaze sharpened. "What's that supposed to mean?"

He tried to look innocent. "Nothing."

"Cooper—"

"Just that any woman who can do a headstand in a wedding dress and then walk down the aisle ten minutes later can pull off anything."

"I can't believe you brought that up!" she sputtered, burying her face in her palm. "I was hoping you'd forgotten that."

"Trust me, that's not the kind of thing a guy forgets. Your legs straight up in the air—"

"Just stop now!"

"Not to mention that cute little pair of underwear with the kitties on them."

She broke off, her mouth open. "What? My…my cute little…what?"

Her cheeks turned bright pink. As bright as her panties had been.

She looked delightfully flustered. Which was not the end goal, now was it?

If she knew how hot she looked, how much he wanted her, she'd boot him out of her hotel room and refuse to so much as look at him again.

Why had it seemed like a good idea to bring up her panties? Right, because he was going tease her. Playfully.

"Those pink panties of yours. With the little white cat heads on them?"

"My Hello Kitty underwear? You saw my underwear that day?"

"Hey, you were the one doing a headstand." He shrugged. "What did you call them again?"

"Stop teasing me."

He leaned a bit closer and caught a faint whiff of her scent, a combination of something light and pepperminty mingled with warm chocolate brownie. "I happen to think you could do with a lot more teasing."

She glared at him, but there was no real annoyance in her expression. "What's that supposed to mean?"

"People tend to take you entirely too seriously."

"That's not true at all. I'm a socialite. I spend my life doing volunteer work, shopping and lunching. No one takes me seriously."

"You're the daughter of a senator and part of one of the most influential families in the state. I suspect everyone takes you seriously." Something sad and shuttered flickered through her eyes, and he added, "Whether you want them to or not."

But she seemed to shake it off and said with mock severity, "Well, you should take this very seriously—don't tease me about my Hello Kitty underwear. She's a beloved cultural icon."

He held up his hands in mock surrender. "I promise. From here on out, Hello Kitty is off-limits. Now, do you agree to help me?"

"And if I do this, you'll really help me track down the heiress? And you'll stay in contact with her? Make sure she gets settled into her new life?"

"Yes, I will."

She eyed him again. "I can't make any promises. I can't promise that I can convince the board of anything. All I can do is try."

"I understand that."

"And I certainly can't promise that this hotel of yours will be a success."

"You don't have to promise me that." He grinned. "I know it will be."

She leaned forward then and set her wineglass on the coffee table. "Has it occurred to you that you could just do this yourself?"

"Do what?"

"Get financing on your own. Buy Beck's Lodge. Start

a whole new company that's independent of Flight+Risk. You could do that."

"I don't want to do that. I started Flight+Risk. It's my company. The board should trust me. They should trust my judgment."

"So basically, you're just being stubborn?"

"No, I'm—" Then he paused, tilted his head a little to the side as if considering the matter and ultimately smiled. "Yeah. Maybe."

"So this is worth it for you? Spending all this time and energy just to prove to your board that your idea is valid?"

"Yes, damn it." Somehow he managed to smile while conveying the depth of his conviction.

He was so sure of himself. So completely confident that she couldn't help but be drawn in by it. Still, did he know why he was really doing this? Did he get it?

She'd done the research on his board over the years—it wasn't just nosiness on her part. With all the fund-raising she did, she considered it part of her job to know as much as possible about everyone and who their connections where. The curse of being a politician's daughter, she supposed. Of course, at some point, mere research had been eclipsed by her natural fascination with complex human relationships.

Robertson had been a member of the board since Flight+Risk went public. He had the perfect background for the position and Cooper had chosen the man himself. Despite that, they had a history of clashing over the direction of the company. Cooper was a natural risk taker and he just couldn't resist rebelling against authority, even when that authority was his own board.

Still, it didn't take a degree in psychology to figure out the real reason he was desperate to get their approval for his pet project. Several members, Robertson in particular, were men of Hollister's generation. In fact, Robertson might as well have been Hollister; the only difference was that he'd made his name in retail instead of oil. Yes, this was a matter of pride for Cooper, but it was also deeply personal. He didn't just want the board's approval. He wanted his father's.

But Hollister was an ass and that bridge had burned down long ago, ignited from both ends. Cooper could never earn his father's approval. Hell, he could never even ask for it. But he could damn well get the board's support if he tried hard enough.

And, she supposed, she might as well help him get it. "If you really want the board to buy into the idea, you don't sell it to them directly. You find outside investors."

"Flight+Risk doesn't need more investors. We've got the money and the line of credit. I just need the board's approval."

"I know. That's what I'm saying. If you want to get their approval, the way to do that is to convince them that you don't need them. That you have other people interested in investing. Not in Flight+Risk, but you personally."

"So I sell them on the idea by not selling them on the idea?"

"Exactly."

"Okay. How do I do that?"

"Well, we talked about inviting the board up to the resort and show them how much potential it has, right?"

"Yeah. Once they see the powder—"

"No, they don't need to see the powder. If your board is like every other board of directors I've ever met, they don't snowboard. Maybe a couple of them ski. They're in their sixties. They've got power and money, but they're not athletes."

He smiled wryly. "You realize you're making sweeping generalizations about people you've never met, right?"

"Am I wrong?"

"No."

"Okay, so just accept that they don't care about the powder. None of the investors will. All they'll care about is whether the snowboarders—the potential clients—care about the powder. So you invite every snowboarder you know out for an exhibition. You plan a fabulous weekend to woo the investors."

"And I invite the board members."

She cocked her head to the side, considering. "No, not right away. Remember what you said before? About not seeming desperate? That's what we're going for here. We want them to think that you can make a go of this without Flight+Risk. You don't pander to them. You invite other people. Rich, important people. People involved in real-estate investment. That type." She thought for a moment and added, "Preferably people who know a few of the board members. What you want is for the word to spread to them via some other source. You want to make this seem like such a sweet deal that the board comes to you. And in order for that to happen, you have to make them think you don't need them at all."

He nearly laughed. "Well, that's easy. Not needing people is one of the things I do best."

She gave a bark of laughter. "See, you're a Cain after all." Then she tilted her head to the side and asked, "Has it occurred to you that the easiest way to get the money isn't to convince the board at all? It isn't even to find investors."

"It isn't?"

"No. The easiest way to get the money for this project would be for you to just find Ginger and win this damn challenge your father set up." He opened his mouth to protest, but she held up a hand. "I know you don't really want the money, but I also know that Griffin and Dalton have both told your father that if either of them win, they're still splitting it three ways. Or rather four ways, since Ginger will get her share, too. Even if you only take a quarter of the money, you'd still have enough to buy this hotel or a hundred hotels."

"You don't get it. I don't want a penny of that man's money. Ever."

"So what are you going to do once we track down Ginger? When the DNA test confirms she's Hollister's daughter—"

"If the test confirms it."

Portia shook her head. "No. It will confirm it. I'm sure. She looks just like a Cain. When you see her, you'll know what I mean." She said it with so much conviction, even he was starting to believe this woman Portia had stumbled across might be the heiress. "So what are you going to do with the money?"

He shrugged. "Give it to Caro, like you suggested."

"Even if she's thrilled about screwing over Hollister, I doubt she'll take all the money. There's bound to be some left over. Easily enough for this."

"I'll convince her," he said grimly.

"You claim you don't want it, but are you really going to walk away from hundreds of millions of dollars?"

"Dalton and Griffin can keep the money. So can this girl, if she wants it."

"This girl who's your sister."

He narrowed his gaze.

"I'm just saying. Because I've never heard you actually call her your sister."

"Your point?"

"I just want to make sure you remember that. She's your sister. And she needs you. That should matter to you."

Then she leaned forward slightly and for a second she

was close enough he got hit with the scent of her, sweet and fresh. Suddenly he was aware all over again how scantily dressed she was. And that they were alone. And that the last thing he wanted to be doing was talking about his stupid family crap.

"I know you don't get along with the other Cains," she said. "But you might decide Ginger is different. You might actually like her."

He didn't quite know what to say to that. He wasn't in the market for a sister. He didn't particularly want the family he already had. Still, part of him knew that Portia was right. He might actually like this girl. And she would undoubtedly have a hard time of it. In all honesty, the best thing for Ginger would probably be to live out her life without ever knowing who her father was. But there was no way that would happen. Eventually Dalton or Griffin would hunt her down.

Whether he wanted the money or not, maybe finding her first would be the best for everyone. Just so long as it didn't take too much of his time or energy.

This Beck's Lodge deal was his top priority. Flight+Risk was his top priority pretty much always. He didn't need any distractions—not the kind a sister would provide and not the kind Portia would provide, either.

But Portia wasn't interested in him. Not really. Yes, she probably felt that spark of attraction that he felt, but he wasn't even sure if she'd admitted that to herself yet. And she wasn't the kind of girl who would ever act on that attraction.

There were rich women who played with professional athletes like it was a hobby. Something they did in their spare time. Portia wasn't that kind of woman. Headstand or not, she was better than a quick and mindless affair. And if he slipped up and made a pass at her, she would bolt. And as of right now, she was too important to him to scare off. He needed her. If he was going to pull this off, he needed her. Badly.

A fact he'd have to remind himself of constantly when they worked together. Which was probably why he shouldn't be lounging around in her hotel room late at night.

He stood. "I'll pick you up first thing in the morning and take you out to Beck's Lodge."

She frowned, using her phone to check the time. "How long will the trip take? I'd rescheduled my flight to Tahoe for tomorrow afternoon."

"Just give me all day tomorrow." That would give him all of tomorrow to convince her to stay much longer.

Five

Portia had her doubts the next day. To begin with, until Cooper pulled up at the private airstrip, she hadn't considered how they were going to get to the resort. Cooper had chartered a flight to take them to Salt Lake City. From there, it had been an hour drive through the foothills and mountains before they turned off on a private road that wound through snow so bright it made her eyes ache.

Traffic thinned and then disappeared entirely. They appeared to be driving through a land completely uninhabited. But then they turned a corner and the lodge rose up out of the surrounding forest.

"Oh, you have got to be kidding me," Portia muttered as she gaped at the lodge.

He grinned at her. "Yeah. It's a beast of a building, isn't it?"

Cooper stopped the car in the circular drive in front of the building. "Come on, let's go take a look," he said as he climbed from the car.

She clambered out of the car after him and headed for the front of the house, practically bounding up the path, she was so excited.

"Don't we need to wait for a Realtor or someone?" she asked once she reached the steps.

"Nah. I talked to the sales agent and the owners this morning and let them know I was coming up. I'm the only one even looking at the property, so they're giving me a lot of latitude. If you want to meet with them later, they'll come on out, but for now we're alone."

Portia stared up at the building squatting on the road ahead, mouth agape. Building? House? Lodge? Monstrosity? It defied description.

Nestled up against the mountain, built of massive wooden beams and rounded river rocks—some the size of VW bugs—it wasn't so much a lodge as it was a monument. It was three stories of sprawling ego and hubris.

"You didn't tell me it was Bear Creek Lodge," she murmured breathlessly.

Cooper pointed to the cheesy sign planted near the driveway. It was made out of fake wood, with carved letters painted bright yellow, like a sign you'd find in a national park sixty years ago. The sign read: "Beck's Lodge, family owned and operated since 1948."

"Not Bear Creek Lodge. Beck's Lodge," Cooper said.

"Do you know the history of this house?"

"I know this is the best powder on the mountain. I know there's no other location that's anywhere near this perfect. Those are the things I care about."

"But you don't know anything about the house?"

"No." He looked at her, clearly baffled. "Do you?"

"Um. Yeah." She turned her hands up in an exasperated gesture. "You want to buy this place and turn it into an upscale resort and you don't even know the history?"

"What history?" He pointed to the sign. "It's family owned and operated since 1948. What else is there to know?"

"What else is there to know?" She laughed, a gurgling bubble of hysteria. There was so much to know. Among some circles, this house was famous. Either the Realtor listing it hadn't done her research or—more likely—no one thought a snowboarder like Cooper would care about the building's unique history. "There's an American author named Jack Wallace. Wallace became famous writing adventure stories set in the American West and during the Yukon Gold Rush around the turn of the century. The turn of the last century, not this one."

"I know who Jack Wallace is," Cooper said drily.

"Well, then you know how he was larger than life. You probably read his novel *Lost at Bear Creek* in school, right? He was one of the first writers to be a worldwide celebrity. He was a millionaire, which, trust me, meant a lot more in those days than it does now. He bought all this land. Thousands of acres. And in 1910 started building this huge house."

"This house?"

"No. Not this house. Wait for it." She shot him a look, surprised that he seemed to be genuinely interested. She was a history buff. And an old building buff. Not many people had the patience to listen to her rattle on about either, but Cooper seemed glued to the story, and she couldn't help reveling at having a captive audience. "They finished the house in 1923 and it burned down, two weeks before he and his wife moved in. This was before the age of insurance. But Wallace refused to give up. He had them start from scratch. The result was Bear Creek Lodge. The remains of the old house are still standing in the national park, which he donated. But by the time he finished construction, his liver was failing and he lived in it for less than a month before he died. His children inherited the house, but couldn't afford to live here because of the taxes. They couldn't agree about what to do with it and eventually it was auctioned off for back taxes. Which I guess is when the Becks bought it."

As she spoke, she took in every line of the house. This crazy, beautiful building, with its blunt Arts and Crafts style angles and its sharp edges. The house seemed to rise up out of the mountain like some sort of ancient shrine. It was beautiful. Despite its state of disrepair. Despite its age. Despite the attempts the Becks had made to brighten it up, with yellow paint and cheap plastic flowers stuck in the ground in front. It was pure folly.

And in some ways, it reminded her of Cooper himself. It was strong and stubborn and deeply rooted in the outdoors. It was larger than life. The stuff of dreams. Deeply appealing without being soft or pliant. This was a house that wouldn't budge, and she sensed Cooper was the same.

He may think he loved this location because of "the perfect powder," but she knew it was more than that. On some level, he connected to the house, too.

"How do you know all this?" Cooper asked from beside her.

"History of American Architecture class. I was an architecture major for three semesters."

"Why'd you quit?"

She sent him a smile and started walking up the front steps of the lodge. "Because no one builds houses like this anymore."

Listening to Portia wax poetic about the building, Cooper couldn't help wondering what he was missing.

Her enthusiasm was adorable, really, and completely at odds with how he thought of her. Sometimes he felt as if there were two Portias, maybe more for that matter. There was the cool and sophisticated socialite who'd been married to Dalton. Beneath that, there was this bubbly, charming Portia, who seemed like so much fun. She was like a Russian stacking doll. Each layer was different from the one inside. Were there any more layers he hadn't uncovered yet? "You know it's really ugly, right?"

She glared at him. "No. It's really beautiful. You're just blinded by the snow."

Was she pretending to be offended or had he actually insulted her? "The inside is dated and hopelessly dark. It's grimy."

"Are you trying to talk me out of helping you?"

"I just want to make sure you understand. I'm turning this into a resort. Not a national monument to Bear Lodge."

"Bear Creek Lodge," she corrected him absently, her eyes still moving restlessly over the exterior of the building.

Suddenly he was glad that he'd asked the Becks to give him time alone to show her the house. He didn't want anyone there while they discussed it.

"No, no. I know." She stepped through the doorway into the lodge and it seemed to take her breath away. "Oh, my."

The door opened right into the great room. There was a reception area with a front desk made of Formica. It was a massive, sprawling room whose ceiling was two stories up. At one end of the room, a river rock fireplace crawled up the wall. At the other, a staircase spilled out from a second-floor hallway. There were a dozen guest rooms up there.

The place was a wreck on every level. But it was big and that counted for a lot when it came to hotels. Still, how would it look through her eyes? Through the eyes of those rich investors she wanted to lure here? They would see the cheesy Formica and the bright yellow paint. Not the perfect snow and endless potential.

"Eventually we'll have to gut the interior and—"

Portia whirled on him and socked him in arm. "If you touch so much as an inch of this interior without my permission I will hunt you down and hurt you."

He rubbed his arm and faked a wince. "Ouch."

"Except that desk. After you buy this place, you can take that out the same day if you want."

"*If* Flight+Risk buys it. If we can get the board to see our side of this."

"I am no longer worried about that." The gleam in her eyes was almost maniacal. "When we're done here, the board is going to be salivating. And you know why?"

"I'm guessing it's not because of the perfect powder," he said wryly.

"No. Not the perfect powder. You've got that angle covered already. And don't get me wrong, it's a good tack to take. But I'm going to play the irreplaceable slice of history angle. That's something that no stuffy businessman can resist. I'd bet you half of these businessmen grew up reading Jack Wallace books."

"You may be overestimating the intelligence of these men."

Her lips curved in a smile. "Maybe. But at any rate, Jack Wallace's books defined what it meant to be an outdoorsman in America. His stories influenced everything from the settlement of Alaska to the development of the national park system. We just have to remind them that snowboarding is part of that tradition."

"You know that actual snowboarders don't care about any of that, right?"

"You worry about what snowboarders want. I'll worry about the pretentious old men with money and what they want." She ran her toe over the dark green floral pattern in the carpet. "Have you looked under the carpet?"

"No."

"It's probably hardwood. They didn't have wall-to-wall like this when Bear Creek was built. I'd guess this was added sometime in the eighties."

Her voice had taken on a dreamy quality. As if the house entranced her.

"At some point, if we do convince the board to pony up the money, there will have to be massive renovations. You know that, right?"

She swatted away his question. "How many bedrooms upstairs?"

"The Becks have rooms on the third floor in what used to be the servants' quarters. Then there are nine bedrooms on the second floor. But only three bathrooms. There are twenty-four cabins, but they're—"

"I don't care." Her voice sounded dreamy, but her eyes sparkled with delight. "This place is perfect."

"It's a wreck."

"No. It's beautiful."

"It's dark and dingy."

"Which we can fix with the right tricks." She whirled around to look at him. "You've already talked to the owners about renting this place for a weekend for the event, right?"

"Yeah. I did that first thing this morning. They're on board."

"And they're willing to let us make superficial changes?"

"They've said that anything we're willing to pay for, they'll let us do."

She eyed him, making him think she was sizing him up. "You're going to pay for this out of your pocket?"

"If I have to."

"Think I can talk you into pulling up the carpet and having the floors redone?"

Right now, when she was looking at him with the gleam

in her eyes, that pure fiery determination, she could probably talk him into anything she wanted. Her unabashed enthusiasm charmed him. It had been years since he'd seen her this excited about something. He loved the way her lips tilted upward as she spoke. How her eyes sparkled. "This is how you always end up talking me into donating to all your crazy causes."

She propped her hands on her hips, looking indignant. "My causes aren't crazy!"

He chuckled, tucking a loose strand of hair behind her ear. "Relax. I'm just teasing." Then he frowned with mock seriousness. "Your causes are very important. Your ability to coax money out of me—that's crazy."

She frowned. "I don't coax that much money out of you."

Oh, she had no idea. He wasn't a particularly generous man. I wasn't like he went around looking for ways to get rid of his money. But every damn time she called, he couldn't resist. Talking about some charitable cause was the only time she dropped her guard. So, yeah, he literally paid money to see her smile. Sucker.

Suddenly, he realized he was still standing close to her. His fingers were still playing with a silken strand of her hair. He dropped his hand and stepped back.

"Yeah. We can cover getting the floors redone."

Her smile widened into a full-fledged grin. She turned around, taking in the entire room. "If we get rid of the carpet, the curtains and most of this god-awful furniture, this place will be amazing. In four weeks, you won't recognize this place."

"In four weeks?"

She turned to look at him. "You didn't honestly think I could pull this off in less time than that, did you?"

He blew out a breath, doing the math in his head. In four weeks, it would be late March. The snow should still be good. They'd be cutting it close. But it would probably take that long alone to get the exhibition lined up. "Okay. Four weeks. I expect miracles."

"Even in four weeks, I can't pull off a miracle. It'll be mostly staging. And we'll have to get the Becks' approval."

"The couple that ran the lodge when it was still open are too old. Their children are desperate to sell this place. I don't think we're going to have to worry about getting their approval for the things you mentioned."

"Of course they're desperate. Bear Creek Lodge has a reputation for being tainted by misery and failure. It's quite the albatross to be saddled with." She wandered into the center of the room and stared up at the ceiling, slowly spinning around before glancing over at him. "And we have the place to ourselves?"

Her voice was pitched low with excitement. Intellectually, he understood the question. She was asking if there were other quests around. But his body heard a whole different question. Were they alone? Would they be interrupted?

He told his body to shut the hell up and leave him alone.

"The lodge hasn't been opened all season. The Becks' children have had it on the market this whole time."

"Perfect. I want to explore."

And before he could stop her, she dashed off up the stairs to take inventory.

Six

Five hours later, they were having dinner at a restaurant in Provo. Portia had three different notebooks open in front of her—thank goodness she'd had spares tucked in her bag. Each notepad had a different to-do list on it. A piece of cherry pie sat off to her left with a cup of herbal tea beside it. She was still picking at her fries and the ice cream on her pie was starting to melt, but she didn't care.

Cooper sat across the booth from her and fiddled with his iPad. He'd already eaten his hamburger and pie and his plates had been cleaned. He must have the metabolism of a racehorse, because he seemed to inhale food voraciously. How on earth did he eat that much and maintain those washboard abs? Not that she knew his abs were tautly muscled. It was just really easy to imagine that they were. Not that she spent tons of time imagining his abs. Or remembering the way he'd played with her hair as he was teasing her.

No doubt about it, Cooper could lay on the charm like

nobody's business. No wonder he had such a reputation as a ladies' man. Apparently, he couldn't turn off the charm. All the more reason for her to ignore that completely.

She flipped from one page to the next and gaped at the growing list. "Okay, you're inviting all the snowboarders, so I don't need to have anything to do with that."

"Exactly," he said. "I'm going to put Jane to work on it first thing in the morning."

"You can have Jane finalize travel plans, but you should call the talent yourself. Just like you're going to call the investors."

"I am?"

"Absolutely."

"Is that necessary?"

"Yes." She smiled reassuringly. "You're a man who throws himself off mountains for a living. Don't let a few investors scare you. Besides, I'm only going to have you call the ones you either know or have some connection to. If it's someone I know, I'll contact them myself before the invitations go out."

"Someone you know?"

"Sure. And I know a lot of people in real estate. Isn't that why you asked me to help?" She chuckled at the dazed look on his face. She flipped her notebook back a couple of pages and pushed it across the table, turning it around to face him. "Look, it's not that bad. You only have to call the ones with the red stars beside their names. It's all people you've met. You phone them, just like it's a social call, and casually mention the exhibition. Don't mention investing at all. Just be friendly."

He studied the page for a moment and then looked up at her with a teasing smile. "Am I supposed to be able to read this?"

She felt a little flutter in her belly. It would be so easy

to get lured in by his charm. So easy, and so dangerous. She forced her gaze away from his face back to the notebook. "Yeah. I guess my notes are illegible, huh?" The table was just a little too wide to comfortably reach across it, so she wiggled out of her side of the booth and slid in next to Cooper. She looked down at the page in front of him. It was a bit of a complicated mess of web brainstorming she'd done. She traced her fingertip along the writing as she spoke. "Here we are on this side of the page. You. Me. You said Matt Ballard and Drew Davis voted in your favor so I included them on this side. By the way, you've already talked to them right? They're available?"

"Yeah. They're in."

"Good, because I can't wait to meet Drew Davis."

Cooper's mouth turned down at the corners. "Ah. Another Drew Davis fan."

"Oh, my gosh, yes!" She could feel herself getting a little bouncy, which she did when she got worked up. "I loved his interview with Anderson Cooper after his visit to the White House. He's so smart."

"Are we talking about the same Drew Davis?"

"Drew Davis the environmental activist?"

"Drew Davis the snowboarder."

"Yeah. I guess he did get his start snowboarding."

"Get his start..." Cooper sputtered, then exhaled slowly. "Drew Davis is the most important snowboarder of his generation. He practically started the sport in America. He..."

"Hey, calm down." She gave him a surprised look. He sounded offended. She bumped her shoulder against his playfully. "I just meant that I know him more for his work with Save Our Snow. I just think it's really cool that he's trying to inform winter sports enthusiasts about environmental issues. It's a good cause. That's all I meant."

Cooper was still frowning as he said, "You know

Flight+Risk had the first board on the market made from ninety-five percent postconsumer recycled material."

She frowned because Cooper still sounded grumpy. Jealous almost. Which was ridiculous, of course. Unless she'd wounded his ego, first by discussing Drew Davis and then by gushing too much about him.

"Oh, I'm sorry," she cooed in baby tones. "Did I offend you?" She put her hand on his arm and rubbed it. She meant the gesture to be silly and teasing, all mock solicitude. But the second she touched him, she was strangely aware of his strength. Was he just super tense or were all his muscles this…steely? Because even through the fabric of his shirt, it was like touching finely hewn wood. And his arm was so big. Massive compared to hers. Her fingers barely wrapped around it. She'd always thought of herself as a sturdy woman. She was taller than average, nearly five-nine, and fairly athletic. But she felt darn near petite compared to him.

And then, suddenly, she was aware that she was still touching him. That her hand was still rubbing slowly back and forth along his arm. And somehow they both seemed to have stopped breathing completely.

Which was probably for the best, because even without breathing, she could smell the faint hint of his soap. Something woodsy and fresh that smelled so good she wanted to just bury her nose against his neck. Which might be the only thing more awkward than sitting here rubbing his arm endlessly.

Or maybe she would just pass out from being so lightheaded. Yes. That would definitely be the best. Then she could excuse her strange behavior as some sort of aneurysm. She waited for several heartbeats. Just in case she conveniently lost consciousness.

"Portia—" Cooper began, his voice sounding unexpectedly husky.

She didn't give him a chance to finish, but plunged back into her explanation of her notes, talking at breakneck speed to circumvent any possibility of him interrupting. "And then on this side we have each of the nine board members who voted against you. These bubbles around their names are other things they're involved in. Business ventures, companies, well-known charitable organizations. Anything one of us might have a connection to."

She had to pause there to take another breath, because—OMG—she might really pass out now.

"Portia—"

Again she didn't let him get in more than a single word. "So for example, here's Robertson up at the top. You said he was your biggest opponent. He has ties to March's department stores, right? And Bermuda Bob's and Mercury Shoes, because he's on their boards. And Hodges Foundation, because he donates heavily to them. The idea is we need to find anyone we know that also knows Robertson. We're not going to invite Robertson himself. That would be too obvious. Instead, we invite other people. People who will spread the word back to Robertson that you're doing this on your own and that it's going to be a huge success. So we need to look at all the things he's involved in and—"

"How did you find all this out?" Cooper asked.

She breathed out a sigh of relief. Thank goodness he wasn't going to question her excessive arm stroking. Finally, a question she could answer. "Google. And a few phone calls. But mostly Google."

"That's a little alarming."

"Says the man with thirty-four thousand search results."

"You did a Google search on me?"

"Well, duh. By the way, you had quite the adventurous

youth. That scandal with the Swedish model and the photographs of your Olympic medal…wow."

He scowled. "That was not nearly as big a deal as it seemed."

"You were reprimanded by the Olympic Committee," she teased. "Sounds like a big deal to me."

"Apparently, they take their medals very seriously."

"Apparently." She had vaguely remembered the incident when it happened, but that had been right around the time of her first miscarriage, so she hadn't been following the news much. But reading a decade's worth of gossip about him had been…enlightening. An endless array of models had paraded through his life. Each more perfect and beautiful than the last.

The Cooper she knew—the easygoing charmer—was vastly different from the ladies' man the media wrote about. It was a nice reminder for her. This guy she was hanging out with wasn't the real Cooper. Maybe that guy with the Swedish model wasn't the real Cooper, either. She didn't know. Either way, she couldn't let herself become lulled by this false sense of intimacy. She couldn't let herself get drawn in by easy charm and his well-hewn arms. She wasn't the kind of woman he went for. He went for Swedish models who cavorted in fountains, naked but for the Olympic medals around their necks. And with wholesome American models who looked fantastic in Flight+Risk jackets.

Not that it mattered to her. Her interest in his love life… Well, she was just trying to be helpful, that was all.

"By the way," she began, trying to be circumspect. "And don't take this the wrong way, but…"

"What?" he prodded.

"Well, the thing is—" She poked at her pie again with her fork.

"Yes?"

Dang it. She was being such an idiot. She set down her fork and twisted so she was looking directly at Cooper. Of course, looking directly at Cooper was like staring into the sun. Mere mortals couldn't do it for long without risking being blinded. "You realize this is working against you here, right? I mean, the bit with the Olympic medal and all the models and the partying—"

"I don't date that many models. And I don't party." His tone was dark and grim. Again at odds with the guy she knew. Or thought she knew. "I never partied much. It was all just the way media portrays me. They love a bad boy."

"Exactly." Though he'd been holding some of those models pretty close in those photos for it to be only image. Not that she cared. "It's an okay for a snowboarder. It's even okay for the CEO of Flight+Risk. But for this venture, you need something more upscale."

He eyed her shrewdly and then said slowly, "Yes. That's what you're here for."

"No, I mean..." Couldn't the man take a hint? "I know. I'm here to make the event look good. And I can handle that. The staging, the food, the guest list. I can do that. But none of it will make any difference if you show up that weekend with a Swedish model on your arm."

She cringed at the sneer in her voice. But maybe it was impossible for a normal, human-sized woman to say the words *Swedish model* without sneering.

"Let me see if I've got this right. You don't think I can keep my zipper up for even one weekend? You think I'd actually risk blowing this deal by dragging some bimbo along?"

"You're not known for your long attention span when it comes to women." She reached for his arm again, this time to placate him, not to tease him. "To be honest, it's not just this weekend. You want to pull this off, you need to be—"

She couldn't even say the next bit without cringing again. "On your best behavior." She sounded like her mother. "All month long. Total media blackout, okay? From now until after the vote. No models. No cavorting. Nothing."

"Not just the weekend, huh?" His expression turned so grim, she knew at once he was mocking her. "I don't know if I can do it. No cavorting at all? No models? What about model trains? Would that be acceptable? Like Swedish model methadone."

"Ha-ha. You can laugh all you want, but I had to say it. There's no point in doing this if you're going to blow it at the last minute."

"Exactly how much of a player do you think I am?"

His eyes searched her face and something in his expression made her breath catch in her chest. He was so handsome. Not classically handsome, not like Dalton was. Cooper's nose had an odd bump where he'd broken it, maybe more than once. He had a tiny scar just below his right eye, and another longer one on his cheek. His face looked lived in. Rugged. Like he'd carved out his identity on the slopes that had given him those scars.

He'd lived a lifetime in that face. There was adventure and resilience and determination written on it. And suddenly her fingers twitched to trace each beautiful scar.

God, she was staring. Leaning into him and making calf eyes at him, staring. She had to snap out of it! This was not okay!

She bolted back to her side of the booth. Desperate to put some distance between them. She pulled her notebook back toward her.

"Okay. I'll try," he said.

"I'm not joking about this." She pressed him because his tone still sounded too glib for her taste. And—yes—because she was still so off-balance she didn't know what else to say. "I need you to take this seriously. Your fans may think this behavior is cute, but the board members see it as a sign of your immaturity."

"Look," he said seriously, "I can keep my damn zipper up. All that stuff with the model and the Olympic medal, that was just—"

"All part of your bad-boy image. I get it."

"No. You don't." He exhaled sharply and ran a hand through his hair. "I used to do that kind of thing deliberately. It was my way of thumbing my nose at Hollister and all the other rich jerks who thought I was worthless because I was poor. It was stupid and immature. In my defense, I was twenty-two. But I haven't dated a model since I was twenty-five. I don't do that crap anymore."

For a long moment, she could only stare at him, mutely. Because the facade of the charming playboy had slipped briefly, revealing the man he was underneath. His intensity. His drive. And his courage.

Because she knew—better than most—about all those rich jerks who could make a person feel worthless. How society could ostracize someone for being just a little bit different. Wasn't that what she'd been avoiding her whole life? Hadn't she learned that from a young age? You kept your head down and blended in with the herd and maybe you survived. If you stood out too much, the lions took you down.

"I'm sorry," she said abruptly. "I didn't mean to sound like I was judging you."

"Look, this is what you're here to do." He gave another one of those harsh sighs. "I created this mess. If I have a shady reputation as an irresponsible playboy, then it's my own damn fault. I just need you to understand that that's not who I am. Not now. Yeah, when I was younger, I acted like an ass. I'd won this huge honor and I didn't respect the medal like I should have."

"You don't have to explain."

But he ignored her. "I'd slept with the model—hell, I barely knew her. And she 'borrowed' the medal for a while. I wasn't even there when she took the pictures. I didn't know she'd done it until the pictures were all over the internet and the Olympic Committee was calling me on the carpet."

"It's really none of my business."

"I'm not telling you all this to dodge responsibility. I just wanted you to know."

"Okay." She thought about Cooper as he'd been when she'd first met him all those years ago. He'd been so charming, but even then she'd seen that crazy quality. That feckless arrogance that had gotten him into so much trouble.

It didn't take a genius to understand why he'd wanted to thumb his nose at everyone trying to control him. She couldn't blame him. If she was honest with herself, she admired his courage. Sometimes she wished she'd rebelled more when she was twenty-two.

"Don't feel like you have to justify what happened. It's a miracle you don't have more daddy issues."

He grinned, but she could see the glint of sadness behind his eyes. The regret sugarcoated in charm. Part of her wanted to probe deeper, but it wasn't her business, so when he changed the subject a moment later, she didn't protest.

"So there's one thing this abstinence plan of yours doesn't take into consideration."

"What's that?"

"If we're going to pull this off, we're going to be together a lot."

Suddenly, her heart rate picked up and she was aware all over again of the intimacy of sitting across the table from him. Of the way he seemed to take up so much space. Of the implication heavy in his voice. They were going to be together. A lot. Did that mean that he was as aware of her as she was of him?

"And?" she prodded. Her heart was pounding as she waited for his next words. Heat spiraled through her body, a secret, intimate heat.

"If we're together all the time and if you help me host the event, people are going to assume we're together. People will talk about you."

"Excuse me?" She squinted at him. That's what he was worried about?

"Your reputation is pristine," he said dispassionately. "I don't want you to damage that by associating with me. So if you're worried—"

"Wait, you're worried about my reputation?"

"Sure. A nice girl like you might not want to be seen with a guy like me."

"Yeah. I get it." Geesh. Wasn't that just her luck? Here she was thinking he was irresistible and he thought she was nice. Nice.

Cozy sweaters were *nice.* Shortbread cookies were *nice.* Tea was *nice.*

Nice had been the bane of her existence since she was about twelve when other girls got boobs and high heels and she—since she was so nice—got mosquito bites and ballet flats. Which had gotten her a position organizing the school dance instead of a date to the dance.

All these years later and she was still haunted by *nice.* Only somewhere along the way, the connotation had shifted around a bit to mean cool and unapproachable. Which, as far as her love life was concerned, was just as deadly.

She pulled her notebook back across the table and slammed it closed. "I'm not worried."

"Well, I am," he began. "People will—"

"People will not think that." She couldn't quite bring herself to admit aloud that she knew he couldn't possibly want her. "No one in their right mind is going to believe we're together."

"Why?" He narrowed his gaze as tension shifted into his shoulders. "Because you're too good for me?"

She huffed out a breath. She wanted it to convey indifference, but instead it just sounded pathetic. "Not because I'm too good for you. Because I'm too nice. Too boring to hold the attention of a guy like you."

He leaned back in the booth and gave her an assessing look. "A guy like me?"

"Well, yeah. Cooper, you're world renowned as a connoisseur of women."

He cringed. "I'm not world renowned…."

"Thirty-four thousand hits. That's pretty renowned. No one is seriously going to believe you'd actually be interested in me."

"You don't think I could be interested in you?"

She shrugged, suddenly immensely uncomfortable. He must think she was the most insecure woman ever. How needy could she be?

"Portia, you're beautiful and smart and rich."

Her back stiffened. "I'm not fishing for compliments. I'm being realistic."

"So am I. I'm not complimenting you to stroke your ego. I'm being honest."

"Okay, then be honest about this, too. Close your eyes for a second."

"What?"

"Just do it." She waited until he had. Then she ordered. "Think back to the first time we met. What did you think of me?"

"Portia, this—"

"No. No editing. Just honesty, right? What did you think of me?"

He opened his eyes. "This is stupid. I'm not going to play this game with you."

"Humor me. It was Christmas Eve. Caro had planned a big family dinner. You'd flown in from Colorado. Is this ringing any bells?"

He clenched his jaw, and she wondered if he wasn't even going to answer. Then finally he said, "I don't remember."

"You don't remember the dinner?" she prodded.

"I don't remember meeting you that night."

She nodded, drawing the action out to buy herself time to let the sting fade before she responded. "That's about what I thought."

"How did you know?"

"I didn't. Not for sure. But when we met again the next summer, you didn't seem to remember me. That's the way it is with nice girls. We fade into the background. We're uninteresting."

"So what you're saying—" he took a slow sip of coffee as if he was carefully considering his next words "—is that I couldn't possibly be attracted to you because you don't make a good first impression."

Seven

Cooper leaned back in his seat, stretched out an arm along the back of the booth and considered Portia over the rim of his coffee mug. Was it possible that Portia—one of the most beautiful women he'd ever met—had a self-esteem issue? How was that even conceivable? She was gorgeous. More to the point, she was smart, funny and quirky. Not to mention passionate. He'd heard her talking about Beck's Lodge. No woman who got that excited about hardwood floors could be a cold fish.

He just shook his head. "Nope. It's not possible."

"What?" She looked a little offended.

"I'm not buying it. I don't believe—not for a minute—that there's a red-blooded guy between here and the equator that wouldn't—" Then he broke off because he couldn't think of a polite term for *hit that.* "Just trust me."

She shrugged. "You're wrong. I've seen it too many times to count. There's something about me that men find unappealing. They don't hit on me." She cocked her head to the side, considering. "Maybe it's my name."

"Your name?"

"Yeah. Portia. It's an intrinsically rich, boring name, don't you think? I've always wondered why my parents didn't name me Polly or Paige. Or Peggy."

He nearly snorted in derision. "You could never be a Peggy. Trust me. Peyton, maybe, but not Peggy."

"But see, Peggy is a woman a man would buy a drink for in a bar. She's fun."

"Peggy is a generation older than you. If she's fun, it's because men my age expect her to bake them cookies, not because they want to date her."

She slouched a little in her seat, clearly unable to counter his argument. "It would still be better than Portia."

"There's nothing wrong with Portia."

"But—"

"So your name intimidates some guys. Any guy that's turned off by a woman's name is a jerk anyway. Besides, there are several things you're not considering here."

She frowned. "Like what?"

"For starters, you keep talking about first impressions."

"So?"

"So, I know you. I've known you for over a decade. We're long past the point of first impressions. I've seen you doing a headstand in a wedding dress. I've watched you face down Hollister and Caro over things you thought were important. I've danced with you at fund-raisers. For that matter, I've seen you waxing poetic about musty old buildings."

She arched an eyebrow. "What's your point?"

"Just that I know you better than you think I do. And I know you're not the rich bitch you think your name implies. In short, you don't fool me. I know exactly the kind of person you are."

She looked briefly disconcerted, but then she smiled coolly. "You forget. It's not you I'm trying to fool anyway. It's your board and potential investors. And what they think about me personally is hardly the point. What matters is what they think about Bear Creek Lodge and more importantly, about your judgment."

"No, the original question was whether or not you were okay with people thinking we're seeing each other." She opened her mouth like she was about to talk, but he waved her protests aside. "No, for a second, just forget about whatever crazy ideas you have about how different we are and about your name or your pedigree. Just for a second, pretend my instincts as a guy are correct and that every man who sees us together is going to assume I'd be an idiot not to do everything in my power to get you into my bed."

Her mouth bowed into a perfect O of surprise. Then, slowly, she nodded. "Okay."

"So you're going to be okay with people assuming that?"

She thought about it for a minute and then shrugged. "I suppose so. People have certainly said worse things about me before."

He was about to ask what she meant by that when the waitress returned, tapping the bill against her palm. "You have everything you need here?" she asked, smacking her gum. "'Cause I'm about to go off shift."

He looked across the table at Portia, who could now barely meet his gaze. He smiled slowly. "Yeah. We have everything we need."

He handed a couple of bills to the waitress and didn't bother to wait for change.

It wasn't until they were back at the hotel—after an endless car ride listening to her run through a to-do list long enough to stretch back to his apartment in Denver—before he asked, "What do you think? Do we have what we need?"

She pulled the hotel room key out of her bag and then looked down at her notes again. "Sure." She tucked a strand of hair behind her ear. "I, um…yeah. I think I can get started." She looked delightfully flustered. "I can have a finalized guest list for you by tomorrow and I'll need a place to stay here. Probably in Provo. And I'm not good driving in the snow, so maybe we can arrange a driver. But other than that—"

He cut her off by gently nudging a finger under her chin and urging her to look up at him instead of at her notes. "Yeah. Place to stay. Driver. Whatever you need, you've got. But that's not what I meant."

"Oh." She slowly closed her notebook without looking down at it. "Then what were you talking about?"

"I'm talking about us."

"There isn't an us."

"So you keep insisting. But I need you to understand something. All that stuff about men not finding you attractive is just nonsense. You're gorgeous. And if Dalton didn't make you feel irresistible every day you were with him, then that's his problem. Not yours."

Her mouth twisted into a wry smile. "Thank you. But—"

"I'm not done."

"Oh. Okay."

"I need you to understand something else. I'm not a nice guy. I'm not selfless. I'm not softhearted. I'm not overly generous. When I donate to charity, I do it for the tax break. When I help people, it's generally because I think they'll be able to help me at some point down the road."

She was frowning now, clearly confused by this train of thought. "Ooookay."

Well, if she'd been confused before, he was about to make things worse. So much worse.

He closed the distance between them and pulled her to him. He didn't give her a chance to protest verbally, but pressed his lips to hers. There was a moment of shock. He felt it in the stillness of her whole body. The way her breath caught and her muscles tensed. But she didn't resist. Not even for a second. She held very still while her body got used to the idea.

Then, slowly, her arms crept around his neck and her lips parted.

As for him? His body had been gearing up for this moment for about the past decade. So the second he felt her relax, he deepened the kiss. He moved his lips over hers, slowly coaxing her mouth open. He slipped his tongue into her mouth, learning the feel of her lips and the unique taste of her. She was sweet and tart, like the cherry pie she'd been eating. But her flavor was more complex than that. There was an underlying smokiness. A hint of darkness. His senses had barely registered all of that when she molded her body against his.

Her purse dropped to the ground beside their feet and he instinctively backed her up against the door until she was arching into him. Seeking him with the same desperation he felt.

Damn, but she felt good. Right. Like she'd always belonged there. Her curves were sexy and strong without being outrageous. Her body was sleek and muscular, but feminine in all the right places. There was so much hidden passion here. So many hidden depths. And he couldn't wait to delve deeper into all that complexity. But they were still standing in the hallway outside her hotel room. Which was entirely too close to her bed. And while he had no problem taking her to bed immediately, he also knew that she was not ready for that.

So he pried himself away from her tempting body and took a step back. He ran a hand through his hair, because—frankly—it gave him something else to do with his hands beside touching Portia.

She just stared up at him, her eyes wide and shocked, her lips pressed together like she was trying to seal in the last of their kiss. "What was that for?"

"That was so you'd know."

"Know what?"

"How much I want you."

"You want? Me?"

"I do. And unless you tell me right now that you're not the least bit attracted to me—unless you ask me to leave you alone—then I'm going to pursue you until you want me just as much. I know you're not there yet. I know you're nowhere near ready. But I'm a patient man and I can wait. But I wanted you to know, right now, what's coming. Because sometime in the next couple of weeks, you're going to convince yourself that I'm flirting with you because I'm just a friendly guy. And that every time I touch your elbow or put my hand at your waist or can't resist touching your hair that it's because I'm just stroking your ego. That I must pity you and I'm just trying to make you feel better."

Her eyes had gone even wider by this point and he couldn't resist stepping closer again. He didn't kiss her this time—but he wanted to. Instead, he ran his thumb just under her lip until she opened her mouth again.

"Just remember, I'm not a nice guy. If I'm pursuing you, it's because I want to take you to bed. It's because I've wanted you ever since I saw you doing that headstand. First impressions be damned. Your relationship with Dalton be damned. I wanted you. And I'm tired of waiting."

* * *

Portia stood in her hotel room just inside the door for several long minutes as she processed Cooper's words.

It didn't bode well for her that she hadn't even been able to enter her room under her own willpower.

No, after making the rather startling proclamation that he wanted her—*Cooper Larson wanted her?*—he nabbed the hotel key card from her hand, popped open her door and gently guided her into her room before handing the key back to her and closing the door behind her. Then a second later, he'd said loudly, "Lock the deadbolt."

Only then did she hear him go into his own hotel room, which was right next door to hers. A moment later, she heard the shower crank on and she stood there imagining him undressing and stepping into it. Naked.

Holy crap.

Not only was Cooper Larson naked in the room next door. He was taking a shower. And if the searing kiss he'd just given her was any indication, quite possibly a very cold shower.

Why was it that she'd never given a second thought to him showering before, but now the idea made her head spin?

Well, no mystery there.

Before, he hadn't dropped that bomb on her. Before, he hadn't told her that he'd wanted her for years. What on earth was she supposed to do with that information?

How was she supposed to work with him during the next month knowing that? How was she supposed to concentrate when all she could think about was the way he'd kissed her?

How was she supposed to—?

Portia suddenly realized that she'd started pacing. A familiar buzz skittered along her nerves. Energy all but bounced through her. When was the last time she'd been this wound up?

She hated this. And damn Cooper for making her feel this way.

And here he was, just blissfully taking a shower, like nothing had happened between them. Like nothing had changed at all.

Well, that was bull.

She grabbed her key card off the dresser where she'd carelessly tossed it and stormed out of her room. It took a solid three minutes of knocking on Cooper's door before the shower cranked off and another minute before he opened the door.

He stood there, dripping water, towel wrapped around his waist. For an instant, a smile flickered across his face, like he thought there was a chance she'd come over here to take him up on his bargain. But then he had the good sense to read her expression.

"What. The hell. Was that?"

For a second, he seemed taken aback, but then he grinned. "Just fair warning."

"How the hell am I supposed to work with you now? How the hell am I supposed to do my job when I'm distracted thinking about the fact that you want to take me to bed?"

Concern flickered across his face. "Is this a sexual harassment thing? Because I never meant—"

She waved her hand dismissively. "I know that. And you're not my boss. I didn't mean my job in that sense. I just meant—" She looked around and noticed that she was in his room. Damn it, she was pacing again. What was wrong with her? She forced herself to be still. What had she meant? "What exactly did you hope to achieve by telling me that? Did you think that once we had the sexual tension out on the table, I'd just come over and rip your clothes off?" She glanced at the skimpy towel. At his naked chest, which was so beautiful her fingers ached to touch him.

"Of course I didn't think that," he protested.

"Because that would be really stupid of me." The words sort of sputtered out of her. Apparently, she could no longer form a coherent thought. She took a step closer to him. And then another. "I just mean, I'm not the type of girl to do this sort thing. And it would be really stupid to do it now."

"It would be extremely stupid," he agreed. But his perfect, irresistible lips had begun to curve into a smile and his voice had dropped to a husky purr.

Sure, she hadn't had sex in a long time. And it had been even longer since she'd felt attractive. Since she'd felt wanted.

But that was exactly how Cooper made her feel. Desirable. Irresistible.

And before she even knew what she was doing, she'd taken yet another step closer and plastered her body against his.

Eight

Portia moved before he had a chance to, rising on her toes and pressing her chest against his. He barely noticed her room key dropping to the ground. Her hands burrowed into his hair, angling his head so their lips could meet.

Everything about this surprised him. From the way she took full command of the embrace to the instant heat of her kiss.

After an hour of watching her nibble at a slice of pie, he expected a hesitant peck. After all her talk of being a nice girl, of being the boring one, he expected timidity. He expected another kiss like the one in the hall. He thought he'd have to be the aggressor, that he'd have to gently tease a response out of her. Instead, she was greedy. Enchanting.

Her hands clung to him even as her tongue traced the crease of his lips. She didn't have to ask twice. He opened his mouth to her, nearly shuddering with desire when her tongue, eager and fast, darted into his mouth. She was almost clumsy. There was no artifice to her. No planning or thought. No seduction. Just pure, searing desire. Whatever else he thought about her, he knew this: she was here because she wanted this. Because she wanted him.

The thought that Portia wanted him—that this amazing, smart, unbelievably beautiful woman picked him, got him hard faster than he would have thought possible given that he'd just stepped out of glacially cold shower.

Yeah, sure. He'd taken plenty of beautiful women to bed, but this was different. *She* was different. Because this was Portia. The woman he'd wanted for a third of his life. The woman he'd never dreamed he could have. She was his fantasy. She was the dream that woke him up in the middle of the night, hot and hard and aching. And she was reaching for the towel at his waist with eager hands. If he didn't slow this the hell down, he was going to come the second she touched him.

There was no way he was going to let that happen. This was his dream. There was no way he was going to let her control it.

He grabbed her wrist, stopping her just shy of pulling his towel off.

She paused for a second, pulling back from the kiss. Her eyes were wide with confusion and doubt. Just looking at her made him go rock hard, but at the same time, that question in her gaze slayed him. Still, after everything he'd said to her, she doubted that he really wanted her. After all this, after the very physical evidence of his desire that she had to have noticed, she still doubted.

He opened his mouth to reassure her. There were a thousand things he wanted to say. And every one of them scared the hell out of him. So instead of speaking, he grabbed her other wrist and whirled her around so her back was up against the wall. He pinned her wrists to the wall on either side her of head and crushed her mouth beneath his. She tasted like red wine and cherries. He couldn't get enough of her. He had the heart-stopping, terrifying thought that he'd never get enough of her.

He shoved the thought aside and pressed his body to hers. She was tall for a woman and fit against him perfectly. There was no finagling, no floundering to position their bodies together. There was just her against him. His mouth on her neck. Her hands plowing through his hair and his erection nuzzling the V between her legs. Like they'd been made for one another. Pure perfection.

Her leg crept up to the outside of his thigh, and she bumped against him, groaning as he nipped at her honeyed skin. His hand slipped under her sweater, up over the silken lace of her bra to cup her breast and pluck at her nipple. Her head tipped back, and she let loose a groan that rocked him to his very core.

She arched onto her toes, straining against him. When he cupped her ass and lifted her, she wrapped her legs around his hips, grinding herself against him. Her hands moved greedily over his shoulders and back. He sucked in a breath as he felt her heels kicking his towel aside. That was it. She had on entirely too many clothes. If he was going to be naked, then damn it, so would she.

He might not have intended to push her, but turnabout was fair play. He stepped away from the wall, squeezing her delectable ass as he carried her across the hotel room to the bed. It took only a few seconds to yank the bedspread off. Then he lowered her to the bare sheets. But he didn't follow her down. As much as he wanted to bury himself inside of her, he didn't want to rush this. He'd wanted her for years. He could wait a few more minutes to make sure this was as mind-blowing for her as it was for him.

He undressed her slowly, lavishing attention on every

inch of silken skin. First, he stripped off her cream sweater and pulled off her jeans. The sight of her nearly naked sent desire rocketing through him. Her perfect breasts were encased in a hot-pink bra that matched her panties.

Because she dressed so conservatively, he never dreamed she'd be wearing something so damn sexy underneath. It wasn't hot-pink kitty panties, but it would do.

Somehow the combination of hot-pink silk and her naked flesh cast in the half-light was almost too much. She was too perfect to look at; she had to be felt to be believed. She had to be tasted.

He shimmied her panties down her hips and kissed his way to the sensitive flesh he'd just revealed. He parted her flesh to reveal the delicate bud of her sex. He lapped at her folds, intoxicated. Desperate. Until she was as needy as he was. Until she bucked against his mouth. Then he slipped a finger inside her. And then another. He suckled her bud as she rode hard against his fingers, groaning. Panting. And finally screaming. Screaming his name as she fell to pieces around him.

The sound of his name on her lips as she came was almost too much to bear. He almost came, too. Without her even touching him. Somehow, he managed to hold back, until he'd found a condom and plunged into her. Thankfully, she was still on the brink. The spasming muscles of her sex were enough to send him over the edge. He came almost immediately. Her voice echoing in his ears, her name on his lips.

Cooper woke up early, content with the knowledge that whatever else happened, this bargain he'd made with Portia was the smartest thing he'd ever done.

He had no doubt her plan was going to work. She was going to convince the board that he could get financial backing all on his own, which would win them over more quickly than any of his arguments had. She was going to help him achieve the goal that had dominated the past year of his life. And he'd slept with her.

Now as far as he was concerned, any day he woke up with a beautiful woman in his bed was bound to be a good day, but with Portia, it was different. Because she was Portia. The one woman he'd always wanted and could never have. Now he'd had her. And if he had his way, he'd have her again. As often as possible over the next month.

Which would be plenty of time to get her out of his system. Portia would never fall for a guy like him. She'd made that clear enough with all her jabs about Swedish models. They had no future together. Which was fine. He didn't want a future with her. Or any woman for that matter. No woman he'd ever known had held his attention for longer than a couple of months. Tops. So there was nothing to worry about with Portia. There was no reason they shouldn't continue sleeping together as well as working together. And he had no doubt that she would agree. No one would turn down sex that explosive. That right.

All he had to do was think of the way she'd come against him and he got hard all over again.

Her body was warm and soft against his, her buttocks nuzzling his growing erection. He could wake her up slowly, kissing the back of her neck. She'd make that little sound in the back of her throat, halfway between a yummy noise and a groan.

Except they'd made love twice more in the night and now she was deeply asleep, her breathing deep and even.

So instead of waking her, he propelled himself from the bed and got dressed, heading downstairs for an early morning jog. He'd burn off some of this extra energy and grab breakfast before she even woke up. He'd ply her with coffee and fresh croissants and then make love to her again. He didn't need to wake her up now. They had all the time in the world.

Nine

From the moment Portia woke up in Cooper's bed, it took her less than thirty seconds to get from *Damn, that was amazing!* to *Holy crap, I slept with Cooper!* to *What the hell is wrong with me?*

Cooper was her brother-in-law!

Okay. Not really. Not anymore.

But he had been once and surely that put him off-limits forever. Surely there was some sort of societal rule about not sleeping with former brother-in-laws. Jeez, even Shakespeare had covered it. *Hamlet* made it pretty damn clear. It was like number three on his lists of big don'ts, right after not strangling your wife—*Othello*—and not murdering your houseguests—*Macbeth*. Marrying, flirting with or sleeping with your former brother-in-law was bad news.

Or did that only count if he was an evil bastard who had poisoned your husband and tried to kill your son?

Ugh. This was *so* not helpful.

When had her life gotten so confused?

For that matter, where was Cooper now?

She sat bolt upright in bed and looked around the hotel. He was gone.

Then, she cocked her head to the side and listened carefully, just in case he was in the shower. But nope, there wasn't a peep from that direction. No running water. No off-key signing. No soft, moving-around-the-bathroom noises. He wasn't here.

Was that a good thing or a bad thing?

She looked around the room, sucking in panicky gulps of air. It was good, right? This would give her time to think. To plan. To get her act together.

She scrambled from the bed and yanked on the clothes she grabbed off the floor until she was decent enough to duck out into the hall. The rest she merely tucked under her arm. She found her room key on the floor a few feet from the door. The swath of hallway from his door to hers may have been the shortest walk of shame ever, but she was keenly aware of every step and she didn't stop shaking until she was standing in the shower, hot water washing over her skin. Washing away Cooper's touch.

She stilled for a second then stepped out of the stream of water, shaken all over again. Was that really what she wanted? To wash away his touch?

Shakespearean life lessons aside, it wasn't as though what she'd done was actually wrong. It was just complicated.

And wonderful. Because no man had ever made her feel the things Cooper had made her feel.

She finished rinsing off and dried herself quickly before putting on the first item of clothing she pulled out of her bag—a simple gray dress. She didn't bother to look for the tights or cardigan to go with it. Instead, she tugged her comb through the long strands of her hair, her mind automatically going back to Cooper and the amazing things he'd done to her body.

Which wasn't to say that sex with Dalton hadn't been good. It had been. But with Dalton, she'd had trouble really letting go. She'd always been so aware of everyone's expectations. Even when she was in bed with him, she'd been conscious of the fact that they were supposed to be the perfect couple. She'd never felt free to just be herself. A problem she simply hadn't had with Cooper. Somehow, for the hours she'd been in his arms, she'd let herself forget that he was her former brother-in-law, that there were countless reasons they couldn't have a relationship and that she was supposed to be the nice girl. The boring girl. The girl who never had crazy, reckless sex with a man who was off-limits.

The question was, which of these two people did she want to be?

Before she could ponder that any further, there was a tap on the door.

She felt unprepared to face Cooper, but she couldn't hide in her room forever. But when she opened the door, she didn't have a chance to voice any of the things she wasn't even sure she wanted to say. Cooper immediately took her into his arms and kissed her. His mouth moved over hers with the same surety and passion he'd displayed the night before. Heat poured through her veins, searing away her doubts. After a long moment, he pulled away from her, tucking a strand of damp hair behind her ear.

"I brought croissants."

"What?" she asked stupidly.

"Croissants. Pastries." He raised a hand to show off a white paper bag and gave it a little shake. "Breakfast?"

She looked from him to the bag and back again, all her doubts rushing back to her. "I can't do this," she blurted out.

"You don't do breakfast?"

"No. I mean, yes. Of course I eat breakfast. I mean, this—" She gestured to the two of them. "I've never done this before. The one-night stand thing." Suddenly she couldn't even look at him anymore. Her panic mingled with her embarrassment and the cocktail made her feel almost light-headed. "I've never had a one-night stand in my life. I only had a few serious boyfriends before Dalton and next to nothing since then. I never in my life did anything like this and I'm just—"

Before she could get anything else out, she felt his hands on her shoulders. He gently turned her to face him. "You're thinking about this way too much."

"I am?"

"Yes. Why make this complicated? We're attracted to each other. We get along. There's no reason why we can't just do this for the next few weeks, enjoying each other in and out of bed."

A knot of tension loosened in her chest. "Right," she said softly. "Just enjoy it."

"Yeah." His lips twisted into a half smile. "This isn't rocket science. You said yourself I'm not known for my long attention span when it comes to relationships. Neither of us wants something long-term. Neither of us is expecting forever here, so let's just have fun."

That gave her pause. "Neither of us is expecting forever?" she repeated.

But he must have taken her words as a statement rather than a question. "Exactly. I'm just not a forever kind of guy."

"And you don't think I'm a forever person, either?"

"Come on, you bought into the fantasy once. You know

better than most that happily ever afters aren't real. That forever never lasts."

For a moment she was shocked into silence. How was she supposed to respond to that? What could she say? She couldn't argue with him. She couldn't deny the truth to his words. Her own marriage—the one that was supposed to be so perfect—hadn't been forever. Far from it.

Of course there was only one response she could give—the one he so obviously expected. She forced a smile. "Of course you're right. The idea of love, of forever. That's just—" The word *silliness* had been on the tip of her tongue, but she couldn't force it out. She couldn't make herself say aloud something so antithetical to her ideals. Instead, she waved her hand dismissively. "I mean, if I couldn't make it with Dalton, then I'm not going to make it with anyone, right?"

Even as she said the words, they curdled in her stomach. She didn't want to believe that. Maybe it didn't make any sense at all, maybe she had no evidence in her life to prove that love could last, but that didn't mean she didn't want to believe.

She looked up to see Cooper watching her, his expression pensive. There was something a little…well, almost hurt in his gaze.

Ugh. She'd been an idiot. What kind of fool brought up her ex with the guy she'd just slept with?

She smiled again, and this time it felt a smidge more natural. "See? This is what I mean. I have no idea what I'm doing here. Bringing up my ex? Isn't that a total rookie mistake? Shouldn't I know better? Isn't that completely against the rules?"

His expression softened. "There aren't actually any rules."

"There aren't?" she asked, frowning. Sure she had dated

a little since Dalton, but not much. And she hadn't been with another man. For all she knew, there were all kinds of rules she didn't know about. "Are you sure? Because I'm totally new at this."

"Yeah. I'm sure. Look, I enjoy your company. We have fun together. The sex is great. It would be great if we could just enjoy this. But if that's too weird for you, I understand. No pressure."

She thought about it. Let the idea of this no-pressure, just-temporary, just-fun relationship roll around in her mind. She had never had a relationship like that in her life. There had always been pressure of one kind or another. The pressure to be with the right guy. The pressure to twist herself into the perfect wife.

But in all these years, had any of those things made her happy? Ever?

It made her a little bit sad to think about giving up her dream of having forever with someone. But in a way, hadn't she already done that? When she'd started looking into adopting a child—all on her own, without a husband—hadn't she known that was going to drastically reduce her chances of finding Mr. Right? Sure, there were still men who fell in love with single moms, but she had to be shrinking her dating pool. Besides, if she was diving headfirst into the mothering thing, she was going to be too busy to date for a very long time.

So maybe for now, an easy, no-pressure affair was just what she needed. Maybe she really had been going about this wrong all these years. Maybe Cooper had the right idea after all. The idea was terrifying and exhilarating all at the same time.

"What about Bear Creek Lodge?" she asked.

"What about it? Unless you think you can't work with me now that we're sleeping together, I don't see that anything about the project has changed. There's no reason this needs to be complicated."

Laughter bubbled up in her chest. "You're my boss and my former brother-in-law. It doesn't get any more complicated than that."

"You say the word and I'll back off," he said, his expression suddenly serious. "If it's too weird, we don't even have to work together on the Beck's Lodge project."

She tilted her head and thought about it for a moment, but it didn't take long for her to realize that she didn't want him to back off. Never in her entire life had she felt this desirable. She loved the way he made her feel. She didn't want to stop feeling that way. She didn't want to stop sleeping with him. But despite what she'd said about not being a forever kind of person, she still needed boundaries.

"If we're going to do this—" she began, but then broke off when his face split into a grin. "I said *if*. If we're going to do this, then we need to have a few rules."

He shrugged, sauntering across the room to wrap his arms around her from behind. "I thought we agreed there were no rules."

He trailed a delicious path of kisses along the curve of her neck, making her mind spin. His hand slipped up to her breast. He cupped her flesh, giving her nipple a tweak. That simple gesture, so compelling, so masterful, reminded her of how completely at his mercy she'd been the previous night.

"Oh, there needs to be at least a few guidelines." Her mind was whirling as excitement suddenly buzzed along her veins. "For starters, I need my own room."

"Sure."

The line of kisses on her neck got wetter, firmer, nipping playfully at her tender skin.

"Even if you're here only on the weekends, I still need my own space."

"Only on the weekends?" He stilled, lifting his head.

She turned to look at him. "Well, sure. You have to go back to Denver, right?"

"Back to Denver?" He was looking at her with a puzzled frown.

"Of course. You can't stay here. Not when you have Flight+Risk to run. If you're going to keep your board happy, you have to continue to do your job. You can't drop everything to babysit me."

"No. Of course not. Wouldn't dream of it."

He didn't sound the least bit concerned.

Of course that might have been because he was intent on nudging the hem of her skirt up so he could cup her bottom. A moment later, the dress was gone entirely, along with whatever other rules she'd intended to list. She was sure she'd had more in mind. Things designed to create personal and emotional space between them. But as his hands pushed her panties down her legs and his fingers found the very core of her, she couldn't think of a single one.

Ten

When Cooper returned to Denver on Monday morning, he found staying away from Portia was harder than it should have been. But after all, she'd been right. He did have a business to run. Normally, he worked long hours. The work demanded it. He demanded it of himself. If he didn't expect himself to give Flight+Risk everything he had, then he wouldn't ask employees to do the same. Despite that, as one week bled into the next, he found himself increasingly distracted by Portia.

They spoke on the phone almost every night. The nights they didn't talk, they video chatted. Every telephone conversation was ostensibly about the project, but that didn't mitigate the intimacy of lying in bed at night, listening to her talk about her day. He automatically found himself describing the ups and downs of running Flight+Risk. Maybe it came from her years of marriage to Dalton, or maybe from the psychology degree she swore she never used, but she had a keen understanding of what it took to run a company and manage so many personalities. All of which made her very easy to talk to.

Worse still were the hours the hours they spent video chatting. She insisted he needed to see things like sample fabrics and invitations and that the easiest way to do that was through Skype. Who was he to complain when it gave him the chance to see her relaxed with a glass of wine in one hand, her hair twisted up in an easy knot on the top of her head, dressed in adorable pajamas dotted with snowmen. He never would have thought snowmen could be sexy, but on Portia, they were more tempting than the hottest lingerie.

He delighted in taking them off her over and over again the following weekend when he visited her in Provo. Yes, he was there to check on her progress, but in reality, they spent much of their time in bed. The weekend after that, he didn't even bother going up to Bear Creek Lodge more than once. Instead, they stayed in Provo. There seemed to be an unspoken agreement between them that they would only be together as long as the project lasted. Suddenly, a month didn't seem like nearly enough time.

It was early Sunday morning, before they'd even finished their coffee, he looked up to see her savoring a bite of her croissant. Her eyes drifted closed as she licked the flaky pastry off her fingertips.

She looked delightfully sensual, and it was all he could do not to take her back to bed right then. Instead he skimmed his hand up her bare leg and teased. "Didn't I tell you they had the best food in town?"

She shifted into his touch. "You were right. I will never doubt you again for as long as I live."

The husky promise in her words sent a thrill through

him. It was the first time she'd so much as hinted at anything beyond this month.

She must have realized her meaning as soon as he did, because she stilled instantly, then pulled back. "I mean, for as long as we're together. Which won't be more than a few more weeks."

He studied her, taking in the panic written clearly on her face. "Right," he said grimly.

She scooted off the bed and slipped into the robe she'd dropped on a nearby chair. He scrubbed a hand down his face, trying to wipe off what he feared was a kicked-puppy expression. Man, could she make it any clearer that she was in this for the short-term?

"I didn't mean anything by that." She turned back around, frowning. "You know that, right?"

"Yeah. It's pretty clear."

She laughed nervously. "Good, because I know this can't last. I know that. It's like, the weirdest relationship ever, right?"

"What?"

"You and I. I feel like we're horribly mismatched."

He felt like he'd been sucker punched by her words. Part of him knew he should let it go. Change the topic. Distract her with sex. Anything. But instead, he asked the really stupid question. "Why do you say that? Is it because of Dalton? Are you still in love with him?"

"Dalton?" she asked, sounding vaguely surprised.

"You were with him a long time." Why was he asking this? He didn't really want to know, did he? Just like he didn't really want to know why she insisted on having her own hotel room when he came into town or why she was always pushing him to go back to Denver on Mondays. Clearly, she took this no-pressure fling thing very seriously. Did he really need her to spell it out for him? "And

I know you asked for the divorce, but…hell, I don't know. Just because you couldn't stand to be married to the guy anymore doesn't mean you don't still miss him."

"Dalton?" she asked, her expression shifting from panicked to something more serious. "No. I don't miss him. And I don't love him anymore, either." She was silent for a long moment while she considered. "But I do miss the part of me that married him."

Cooper raised an eyebrow, and she laughed nervously, ducking her head as she tucked a strand of hair behind her ear. At least she didn't look like she was going to run from the room anymore.

"I mean, I miss the innocence and hope that I had when I married him. I miss the girl who thought she had love all figured out. I miss her. I miss being her."

She sounded so sad when she said it. So mournful. And listening to her talk, Cooper actually missed that girl, too. That young Portia, who'd been so full of hope. Jesus, had he ever been that young? Had he ever felt like that? Like he might have love all figured out? No. Not that he remembered.

If it had been any other person, he would have sneered at her sentimentality. But it was Portia. So instead he just wanted to comfort her. To protect her.

"You could get married again," he suggested.

Why the hell had he said that? What if she thought he wanted to marry her? Because, damn, what kind of idiot brought up marriage to a woman he was sleeping with if he didn't want to marry her?

But thankfully, Portia didn't go there. She shook her head. "I think I'm past that stage of my life. I think I'm just done hoping for a happily ever after." She raised a hand to ward off any objections he might have voiced—if he'd been the type to believe in happily ever after. "I don't mean to sound bitter. I'm not. It's just that I tried dating after Dalton. No one was worth the effort. No one wanted the things I do and I'm past twisting my expectations to fit someone else's reality."

"What do you mean no one else wants the things you do?"

"Do you know why Dalton and I got divorced?"

"Because he was a heartless bastard who spent too much time working and never appreciated what an amazing woman you are?"

Her mouth twisted into a half smile and she chuckled a little. As if she didn't really believe the compliment but appreciated it anyway. Then her smile faded. It was like the time-lapse photography version of the way she'd dimmed over the years she'd been with Dalton.

"Actually, that wasn't it at all. I never minded how dedicated he was to Cain Enterprises. I knew what I was getting into when I married him. I knew I'd always come second. It wasn't that. I could have put up with that indefinitely."

"You shouldn't have had to," Cooper said gently.

She ignored him. "But I wanted kids."

"And he didn't?"

"No, he was fine with the idea of kids. We tried for years, in fact. It just didn't work out."

Her head was tipped down as she said it, making her expression impossible to read, but he heard the sorrow in her voice. The unspoken pain. He remembered now—one Christmas when Caro had whispered something about a miscarriage. The implication that it hadn't been the first. And he couldn't help thinking about the toll that had taken on Portia.

"I'm sorry." Sorry didn't begin to cover it. Not even close, but there was so little he could say. She shrugged, something in the movement making him think that it wasn't his sympathy she wanted, but something else entirely. "And that's why you got the divorce?"

"Yes, it is. I wanted to keep trying. He didn't."

"He should have—"

"Don't get me wrong. I don't blame Dalton. Infertility takes its toll on a relationship. It's easy to become obsessed with it. I was so desperate for kids, sometimes I think he was right to put a stop to it. I wanted more and more fertility treatments. Then when those didn't work, I wanted to adopt. He insisted we slow down, take a break. I asked for a divorce."

Her voice was oddly quiet—almost emotionless—as she recounted the end of her marriage. Still, he heard the guilt in her words. She blamed herself, not Dalton, for how things had ended. But Cooper knew the truth—Dalton was a heartless bastard who'd ignored his wife's needs. Maybe that wasn't the whole story, but that was how Cooper saw it.

"He should have been a better husband."

She smiled again. Another one of those smiles that was a little sad and a little wry and broke his heart a little. "That's not the point of the story."

"Okay, then what is?"

"You asked why I didn't think I'd marry again. This is why. While I'm the first person to admit I got too obsessed with it last time around, becoming a mother is still very important to me. After Dalton, I thought I would meet someone else. Someone who wanted kids like I did. That hasn't happened and I'm weirdly okay with that. I don't need a husband to be a mom."

"You're going forward with the fertility treatments," he summed up.

"No. That was what made me so crazy last time. This time, I'm going to adopt."

He sat back in his chair slowly. "I see."

Her gaze darted to his, suddenly sharp. "You do?" she asked suspiciously.

"Yeah." Because this was Portia and she didn't do anything halfheartedly. She held herself coolly distant from something until she'd decided to commit, then she threw herself into it 100 percent. "I'm thinking you're not the type to adopt some rosy-cheeked baby, are you?"

"Of course, I thought about that first. I've been working with an adoption attorney for over a year now. So far no luck."

"Why not? You'll be a great mom."

"Private adoptions are tricky. There's a lot of putting out feelers and then waiting to see if you get any takers. And there are a lot of couples out there trying to adopt. I guess when a woman is looking for the perfect parents to raise her baby, she automatically thinks of two parents. Not just one." She gave a little shrug. But then her eyes took on the glow of excitement. "Which is why I'm thinking about going through the foster care system. Adopting an older kid. There are so many who need homes and—" Then she broke off nervously, as if she'd just spilled a secret she hadn't meant to share. "I haven't told this to anyone yet. I don't know why I'm telling you now."

He leaned back and studied her, marveling all over again that she was just as beautiful at thirty-two as she'd been at twenty-one. And that the more he got to know her, the more attractive he found her. The deeper layers of Portia's personality revealed intelligence and passion, selflessness and sensitivity. Which frankly kind of sucked.

"You were telling me why we made the strangest couple ever." He couldn't help the note of grim finality in his voice.

She didn't seem to hear it though. "But I guess it doesn't matter if this isn't anything more than just two friends who happen to enjoy each other's company in bed."

"Right," he said, suddenly feeling unexpectedly deflated. "Because we were never going to be anything more than a brief fling."

"Exactly," she said, sounding more cheerful than she had earlier. "If I was looking for anything more than that, you would be my last choice."

"Your last choice? Ouch."

"Don't pretend to be wounded. You don't want to be a father. And even if you wanted something longer than this, you and I in a real relationship would be very messy."

"It's already messy. We jumped right past the part where it would have been anything else."

Her lips twisted into a smile. "True, but I've already had my heart broken by one Cain brother. I don't think I'm up for round two."

And that was one argument he couldn't possibly defend himself against, because in the end, she would always be Dalton's ex-wife. Neither of them could outrun that. And she was right. They could never have more than just this month, because he couldn't give her the things she really wanted.

He took another sip of her coffee and then asked, "Is that the real reason you're doing this?"

She turned and looked back at him. "Pardon?"

"Your adoption plans? Are they the real reason you're so desperate to find the missing heiress?"

She frowned. "I don't understand—"

"You're so worried about how she's going adapt to having wealth and social position thrust upon her. You're so desperate to make sure she can handle it. It's not really about her at all, is it? It's about this kid you want to adopt."

"I—" The furrow between Portia's brows deepened as she blinked in confusion. "I hadn't thought about it." Slowly, her shoulders sagged. "I don't know. Maybe it is.

I'm trying to be smart about this adoption thing. Trying to plan ahead and think through all the hidden pitfalls. But in the end, I'm planning on taking some kid out of her world and bringing her into mine. She'll have all kinds of resources that she doesn't have now, but she'll still be living in a world that's harsh and cutthroat."

He couldn't help but smile at that. "If you're adopting some kid out of foster care, there's a decent chance she's coming from a world that's harsh and cutthroat."

"Good point. But at least that world is familiar. She knows the rules. She knows what to expect."

"You're forgetting one thing. She's going to have you in her corner. With you at her back, she'll be fine."

She reached across the table and gave his hand a friendly but dismissive squeeze. "I'm glad we're friends."

Friends? Was she kidding? They'd just had some of the best sex of his entire life and now she was relegating him to the friend zone?

But he was the one who'd worked to sell her on the idea of a no-pressure, just-sex relationship. It was just that he'd never had that with someone he was friends with. Sex with a friend was so much more than he'd ever bargained for. And he couldn't help thinking that whatever time they had left wasn't going to be nearly enough.

With two weeks to go before the exhibition, he actually thought about taking time off from Flight+Risk—not to manage the project, but to be with Portia. He certainly had plenty of vacation days. And, hell, what was the point of being the CEO if he couldn't occasionally take time off to do what he wanted?

The second the thought crossed his mind, he panicked. He'd never once taken a vacation just to take time off. Sure, he went on plenty of snowboarding trips—that was just part of the job, in addition to being the thing he loved best. But there'd never been any woman in the world he'd wanted to ditch work to hang out with. The fact that he felt that way about Portia was enough to send him back to Denver fast.

Not that that put her out of his mind. But he took to emailing her instead of calling. He got the endless stream of texts. Although he tried to keep his answers short, he found himself texting her back, responding not only to her questions about work, but sending her personal messages, as well. Before he knew it, he was text flirting with her, for God's sake.

By the time Thursday rolled around, the first thing he did in the morning was reach for his phone to see if Portia had texted him when she woke up. Like him she was an early riser. Sure enough, there was a text from her.

Made you a reservation at the hotel for Friday and Saturday night. OK?

In fact, it should have been okay. After all, he'd told her he was coming out for the weekend, but the way his heart rate picked up at the idea made him nervous. Before he could analyze his response, another text came through.

Also made appointment for tasting at the bakery on Saturday morning. Ate a croissant on your behalf.

A second later she sent him a photo of a croissant with a large bite taken out of it.

He chuckled at the picture, but there was something else underneath. A pang of longing maybe. He had a day full of meetings and idea pitches—the stuff that was the lifeblood of his company—and all he wanted to do was hop on a plane to Utah so he could feed her bites of croissant.

Annoyed with himself, he typed a quick reply.

Will be off-line most of today. Might not make it out to Provo this weekend after all. Then he added, *Keep the hotel res just in case I need a place to crash.*

Then he tucked his phone into his pocket, determined to not even glance at it again.

He made it precisely eleven hours and forty-two minutes before reading the texts she'd sent him throughout the day. There were a couple early in the day, then a flurry later in the afternoon. Then nothing.

By the time he texted her back that night, he hadn't heard from her in hours. When she didn't respond right away, he knew he should let it go. Instead, he found himself dialing her number.

She answered quickly, but her voice was subdued. "Hi." She gave a nervous-sounding chuckle. "Sorry I flooded you with texts today about the flooring."

"Don't apologize," he said, too harshly really. But why the hell was she apologizing? He was the jerk who'd been dodging her texts. "I was just in meetings all day."

"Sure. No, it's okay. I got it sorted out. The Becks are still being super accommodating. I shouldn't have even bothered you."

"Don't worry about it. I trust you."

"That's just it," she said abruptly. "I know you do. You've got total faith in me. And the Becks, too. Every time I suggest something, they jump right on it."

"They really want to sell," he mentioned.

"They're depending on me to get the hotel in shape for you. You're depending on me to win over investors. Are you sure you should be trusting me with this?"

"Hey, calm down. You're sounding all panicky."

She went instantly silent.

"Why don't you take a deep breath and tell me what's really going on here."

"I don't know!" she admitted. "Suddenly this just all feels very important. You're spending a huge amount of money. You may never see returns on this investment. And basically we're trying to hoodwink your board. This whole endeavor could be doomed. What if we fail? What if I fail?"

"You're not going to."

She gave a little snort. "Yeah, your confidence in me is really great, but you know this isn't *Peter Pan,* right? If you clap long and hard and swear you believe in fairies, that still doesn't mean I'm going to be able to pull this off."

"I don't think I have a response to that," he said.

"Why? Because secretly you know I'm right?"

"First off, snowboarders are prohibited from understanding any and all references to *Peter Pan*. Or any other Disney movie for that matter."

She gave a bark of laughter. "You are not."

"Of course we are. It's in the code."

"The code?" she asked suspiciously. "There's no code."

"Oh, yeah, there's totally a code. We also can't stop and smell flowers or order drinks with pink umbrellas."

From her laugh, Cooper could tell she was beginning to feel less panicked. It was a genuine chuckle, not the crazed bark of laughter that had escaped her a moment ago.

"It sounds like a pretty tough code. What if the bartender gets your drink wrong and puts an umbrella in your Scotch?"

"Well, if that happens you have to just beat the crap out of him."'

"So this snowboarder's code is all about being tough and manly, huh? Is that why you're not nervous about this? Frankly, you should be even more panicked than I am. Is it just that all those years of throwing yourself off mountaintops has deadened your ability to perceive risks?"

He laughed then. "I guess it might seem that way, huh?"

"Yes, it does."

"You know the thing about snowboarding, though? People talk all the time about how dangerous it is. And I'm not going to lie. It is dangerous. But when you're a professional, when you do this for a living, you don't take unnecessary risks. Planning, knowledge, preparation…those are all things that mitigate the risks. Now you can't plan for everything, but you prepare for the things you can and you don't let your fear get in the way. So sure, we all get nervous. We just do it anyway."

"You don't seem nervous," she said begrudgingly.

"Well, that is part of the code. You do what you need to do so you don't let the nerves show. The nerves, they help you focus. They help you commit to the run. You just hang on. But you never let them get in your way." He paused for a second to let his words sink in. "This project at Beck's Lodge, it's the same thing. Sure, I'm nervous. But I'm also ready. I've done the research. I've hired you—and believe me, despite any doubts you're having right now, you are the best at what you do. I'm sure there are plenty of things that will happen in the next month that I can't prepare for, but that's just life."

Again, there was silence on the other end of the line. "You're not saying anything," he prodded gently. "Do you need to go do a headstand?"

"Shut up," she said with a soft chuckle.

"So we're good here?"

"Yeah. I still don't understand how you can be so relaxed about everything."

"Because I've got you working on my team. That's how."

* * *

After her bout of hysteria, she expected him to get off the phone quickly. There was no way he'd want to stay around for more of her crazy cakes, especially not after he'd been distant for so much of the day.

Honestly, she didn't quite know what to make of him sometimes. He was confident to the point of being cocky. He was smart as hell and ambitious. Despite all that, she couldn't shake the feeling that he was also lonely.

She knew better than most how hard it could be to find true friends when your net worth put the county budget to shame. It wasn't easy making friends under those circumstances. Which was why you had to be loyal to the ones you did make. All the more reason for her to step up and protect Caro. And to take care of the heiress.

But what about Cooper? Who was going to take care of him?

They stayed on the phone a few more minutes after that. Quietly talking. Though she'd gotten used to the phone calls from Cooper from her bed, she was still keenly aware of how close she felt, talking to him. Somehow, their nightly chats seemed more intimate than the hours they actually spent in bed. But eventually, they did hang up. She lay there in bed for several minutes after that, just thinking about Cooper.

She'd never had anyone talk her out of a panic attack before. For that matter, she wasn't sure there was anyone other than her therapist who even knew she had panic attacks. And Cooper also knew she was trying to adopt, something only her lawyer and social worker knew. Moreover, he hadn't dismissed the idea.

It felt odd that he knew these secret private things about her that no one else knew.

And it still made her unthinkably sad that he seemed

to not have anyone he was close to. Maybe she had it all wrong. Maybe he really was that emotionally self-sufficient. Maybe that was part of the snowboarder's code. But the more she thought about it, the more she wondered if he didn't need his sister just as much as she might need him.

Later, Portia did what she should have done two weeks ago. She dug through her contact list for the name of a private investigator that her father's secretary sometimes used. Portia had only met the man once. When her mother had learned that she and Dalton were getting a divorce, she'd tried to strong-arm Portia into hiring the guy to dig up dirt on Dalton. Turned out the P.I. was too ethical to go behind Portia's back. She liked the idea of an ethical P.I. Especially one she trusted with sensitive information and whose email address she had handy.

Eleven

It about killed Cooper to stay away from Provo the week before the exhibition. It killed him to be in Denver when his dream was taking place at Beck's Lodge. At least that's what he repeatedly told himself was causing the pain.

His biggest challenge as CEO of Flight+Risk had been learning to delegate. His temptation had always been to do everything himself. Sure, it was hard to keep his ass in Denver where he needed to be. The four times he hopped in the car and made it halfway to the airport before turning around and driving back home were proof of that. But it had nothing to do with Portia and everything to do with the fact that he was a very hands-on CEO.

He limited their contact to emails and to the occasional telephone conversation. Still, most of the phone calls—like the one he was on now—happened late at night, after they'd both had dinner and their schedules were clear.

If he wanted to push his luck, he could say something

licentious. He pictured her blushing. She had the kind of pale skin that blushed beautifully and often. And when she blushed, it tinted not just her cheeks, but her neck and chest too. The thought of all her delicate skin flushed pink with titillation was almost more than he could bear.

"Well, okay then," she said in the cheerful tone she always used as she was transitioning from work talk to anything more personal. "I think that's about it."

"Okay, I'll—"

"No, wait. That's not it. I just remembered. I got an email from Drew Davis yesterday and then he called today to confirm. He said a couple of his friends are going to come up tomorrow to build the slope for the exhibition. They'll be—"

"Wait a second." Cooper sat up in bed. "Did he say a couple of his friends or *The* Friends?"

"I don't know. Why?"

"Because The Friends are a very specific group of guys. They're five of the best snowboarders in the world. They all came up through the competitive ranks about the same time and that's how they got their nickname."

"And Drew is one of them?"

"No, he and I are both about ten years older. Which is why it never occurred to me…"

"Wait, didn't you invite the snowboarders?"

"Most of them, sure. But Drew said he'd invite some guys he knew and I let him handle it." And he'd been too distracted by Portia to follow up and ask whom Drew had invited. It was the first time in his life he'd let work slide to be with a woman. "Damn it, I guess it's too late to do anything about it now."

"You sound stressed out about this. You said these guys are good, right?"

"They're some of the best," he admitted grudgingly.

"If they're coming to help build the slope or whatever and they're going to board in the competition, that seems like a good thing to me. Won't that just impress everyone?"

"Yeah. Sure."

"Then what's the problem?"

The problem was all of The Friends—one or two in particular—were total players.

"There's no problem," Cooper finally said aloud, but only because he couldn't think of anything else to say without sounding like a jealous ass. "Just, you know, watch yourself, okay?"

"Watch myself? What's that supposed to mean?"

"Just be careful. Some of these guys have reputations as womanizers."

"You have a reputation as a womanizer," she pointed out.

"Which I've told you is largely exaggerated."

"Then I'm sure theirs is, too."

Yeah. Well, he was not at all sure about that. In fact, he'd bet money that Stevey Travor was going to show up, take one look at Portia and dial the charm up to eleven. Not that she'd fall for it. At least, not right away. Not while she was still with Cooper.

But they'd both agreed that their relationship would end after the exhibition. And he'd worked damn hard to convince her that no-pressure, commitment-free sex was the way to go. Had he inadvertently primed her for the likes of Stevey Travor?

"Just don't listen to anything they say, okay? And don't spend too much time alone with any of them."

She chuckled dismissively. "I think I can handle it. Besides, it's not like I'm going to be with them. I have things to do. The floor guys will be there tomorrow putting down the final layer of wax. Drew promised me that he was going to oversee everything and that I didn't even have to leave the lodge."

"Drew said that?" Ah, great. This just kept getting better and better. "Drew is coming with them?"

"Yeah. Didn't I say that?"

"No, I must have missed it." However, he didn't miss the implied intimacy of her words. Just how friendly had she gotten with Drew over the course of the past month, when he'd been stuck here twiddling his thumbs in Denver?

"Are you worried they won't do a decent job?"

"No," he muttered tightly. "They're the best. I'm sure they'll do a great job. I'm thrilled they're all chipping in."

He ended the call a few minutes later—before he could make any more of a fool of himself—assuring her he was thrilled with her progress.

And he was. Of course he was. Just like he was thrilled that The Friends had gotten involved. They were some of the hottest snowboarders around. He knew all of them personally and two of them had endorsement deals with Flight+Risk. Their involvement would draw a lot of media attention, as would Drew's. He was glad he had business associates who agreed with his visions enough that they were willing to jump in and help.

He just wished that Portia hadn't sounded so damn starstruck the times she'd talked about Drew Davis. He also wished that freakin' Stevey Travor wasn't coming. Because the guy was notorious. And even though she would never admit it, she was vulnerable to that kind of charm.

Stevey was a scoundrel looking for nothing more than a willing woman. Cooper knew damn well that was exactly the kind of guy who could talk his way into her bed. She'd fallen for it with him, hadn't she?

As beautiful as she was, she'd somehow never learned the power of her own beauty—probably because Dalton was such a class A idiot. Her innocence—combined with her romanticized view of relationships—made her particularly vulnerable to the charms of a guy like Stevey. Or Drew for that matter.

And now that he thought about it, hadn't Drew just finalized his third divorce?

Damn.

There was no way he was leaving her alone up there on his mountain with those two.

Portia hadn't really believed Cooper had anything to be suspicious about when it came to The Friends. First off, she was so busy that she doubted she'd even see them, at least not until they were finished with whatever snow-related job they were doing—which she didn't really understand, despite Drew's attempts to describe it. She had been working twelve-hour days getting the hotel ready for the exhibition and the party the night before. In what little spare time she had, she'd been furthering the search for Ginger. Despite Cooper's doubts, she was still convinced that Ginger was the missing heiress. The information the P.I. had turned up only confirmed her conviction. And Cooper's protests had only strengthened her resolve.

She'd been in contact with Dalton and Laney about the matter and had even called Griffin. They had been intrigued enough by her theory that they had shared the information they'd discovered about Hollister's indiscretion all those years ago. But as eager as Portia was to delve into that mystery, she was still determined to pull off an exhibition worthy of Cooper's ambition, even if she was starting to have doubts about the project.

Of course that was before a pair of passenger vans pulled up in front of the lodge just before lunch. She'd been overseeing the work on the floors, which needed to be waxed a second time and buffed at least twice before anyone walked on them, when she heard the noise. She hurried out the front door only to stop short on the deep wraparound porch.

Each of the vans pulled a trailer with four snowmobiles. The doors swung open and out poured a dozen guys. Or maybe it was fewer—they were all so big. And rowdy. It was hard to tell how many there were exactly.

Drew was the only one she recognized, because she'd seen footage of him when he'd talked at the UN about climate change. Plus, he'd competed in the Olympics on the American team with Cooper, so she'd actually seen him board. Like Cooper, he was all lean muscle, though if she had to guess, she'd say he was an inch or so shorter than Cooper. He wore his hair long and scruffy. Though he was handsome, he lacked the intensity that made Cooper so irresistible.

When Drew spotted her, he bounded up the stairs and gave her a big bear hug like they were old friends, even though they'd only spoken on the phone a handful of times.

"Portia! Great to finally meet you!"

"Um, yeah," she squeaked, even though he'd squeezed all the air out of her lungs. "Nice to meet you—" he gave her another bone-crunching squeeze as effective as a trip to the chiropractor "—too."

As he released her, he laughed like she'd said something funny. "Come on. I'll introduce you to The Friends. They can't wait to meet you."

She surveyed the group of guys at the bottom of the stairs. Some of them were already unloading the snowmobiles, others were unpacking massive bags from inside the vans. While they worked, they jostled and pushed one another like a litter of rambunctious puppies.

Drew called them each over to meet her, as if she could possibly remember their names, when they all looked so much alike—young and handsome, with ruddy, wind-roughened cheeks. Most of them immediately went back to work. A couple hung nearby and seemed to be waiting to talk to Drew about something.

When he introduced Wiley, the cameraman, and Jude, the director, she looked back and forth from the men to Drew.

"Cameraman and director?" she asked. "Aren't they snowboarders, too?"

"Only amateurs," one of the younger guys who hadn't gone back to work interjected. His name was something with an *S*. Scotty maybe? No, Stevey.

"So they're here to..."

"Film the project," Drew said simply. "They've been wanting some footage of what it takes to build a jump. So they'll film us for the next two days. And then they'll film the exhibition, too."

"You know Drew here is going to be movie star, right?" Stevey had edged closer to her and bumped his shoulder against hers playfully.

Drew looked embarrassed. "Hardly a movie star. They're making a documentary about Save Our Snow."

"That's fantastic!" she said. "You know I've been following the work you've done with—"

"You're going to come up and watch us work, right?" Stevey interrupted her.

She nearly smiled when she looked at him. If the other guys were like puppies, Stevey was like an Australian shepherd. He'd started tugging at her heel the second her attention strayed from him.

"I really can't," she said truthfully. "I've got too much to do."

"You have to come! If you've never seen a jump being

formed before, now's your chance. You're gonna love it. I promise."

He might as well have started waving and shouting, "Look at me! Look at me!"

She glanced at Drew for support. "I really—"

"If you're busy, you don't have to stay the whole time. I'll bring you back down the mountain myself."

She looked up at the lodge and then at the vans. It was true that until the floor guys finished inside, there wasn't a whole lot she could do here. "How exactly do we get up there?"

"We'll take the snowmobiles up. Scout out a location and then get started."

"The snowmobiles?" she asked doubtfully.

This was a hiccup she hadn't considered. It had never occurred to her that they would need snowmobiles to get up the mountain for the exhibition. There were over thirty confirmed guests and technically, the event was open to the public. That had gotten them some good press coverage in the local papers.

Frowning, she looked from the snowmobiles to the guys.

"You're coming, right?" Stevey asked again.

"Oh, sure." She nodded mindlessly. It would give her a chance to talk to Drew about this transportation problem. She certainly hadn't come this far to give up now. After all, she hadn't let the debacle with Cooper slow her down. Why would a little thing like snow stop her?

Twelve

Cooper left for the lodge first thing in the morning. He wasn't about to leave Portia alone with those guys any longer than necessary. Despite that, the earliest flight he could get to Salt Lake City wasn't until ten. By the time he took the helicopter from the airport down to the lodge, it was well after lunch. He was annoyed, but not particularly surprised, when he talked to the flooring crew and discovered Portia was not there, but rather off with Drew Davis and The Friends. Of course she hadn't taken his concerns seriously. He hadn't been exactly laying it all out on the line because he hadn't wanted to sound like an ass or an idiot.

But by the time he talked to Drew and figured out where they were, and then borrowed a snowmobile from the Becks and made it up the mountain, he was done worrying about how he looked.

When he pulled up, the guys were almost done building the jump.

Something in his heart clenched when he saw Portia. She was dressed in her bright pink ski gear, looking like she'd planned on staying out for several hours. She looked ridiculously adorable among all the rugged guys. Pale blond hair in braids on either side of her neck peeked out from beneath her snow cap. Her cheeks were rosy, her eyes hidden behind oversized sunglasses. She looked like Heidi by way of a *Vogue* photo shoot.

She waved when she saw him, but her smile froze. "I thought you weren't coming up for a few more days," she said as he shook hands with Drew.

Drew was the only one near her. Cooper recognized the director and cameraman from a previous meeting, but they were both focused on filming the other guys.

"I had an unexpected opening in my calendar." Drew was standing closer to Portia than Cooper liked, so he stood on her other side, casually dropping his hand onto her shoulder. "So I decided to come on over and keep an eye on things."

Drew grinned as if he saw right through Cooper. "Hey, things are fine, man. You have nothing to worry about."

Cooper nodded toward the jump. "Sure, you and The Friends are experts at this, but sometimes you need a more delicate touch."

"You don't think I have a delicate touch?" Drew asked.

"I just think I have a little more invested in this than you do."

Drew threw back his head and laughed. "Good point, man. Good point. But don't worry, I'm watching out for your interests here."

Portia was looking back and forth between the two of them, her brow furrowed in confusion. Apparently, she'd missed the entire subtext of the conversation. Which frankly relieved him. He didn't need her to know how tied up into knots he was over her.

Portia practically beamed at him. "Do you see what they're doing?" She pointed off toward the jump, rising up and down on her toes. Either she was very cold or very excited. And it was adorable. "They've been building the slope all morning. They actually moved the snow from over there—" she pointed off to her left "—to over here. In big blocks like bricks. And then they packed in the rest of the snow to make it swoopy like that."

"Swoopy?" he asked.

"Yeah. Swoopy." She made a motion with her hand that could only be described as…well, swoopy.

"It's a jump, not a slope. And that's the kicker, not the 'swoopy part.'" He shot Drew a glare. "Have you been letting her call it a *slope* and a *swoopy part* all morning?"

Drew just flashed her a charming smile and threw an arm around her shoulder. "It's adorable."

"Oh." For a second, she looked embarrassed, but then she waved it away. "Anyway, it's amazing to watch. I had no idea they were going to do this."

Cooper shrugged. "This is how it's done."

"I think I expected more machinery to be involved or something."

"Nah, real snowboarders don't want anything messing with their powder."

"It's a lot of work," she said. "All these guys must really like you for them to come all the way here to do this for you."

He looked at the jump. They were already smoothing out the snow on the kicker, dragging the backs of snow shovels down the curve. The kicker was nice and tall, so they'd have a ton of air when they jumped. They would put on an amazing show.

"Nah," he said. "They would come do this anywhere, anytime, if it meant they'd get to ride it later. That's the thing about these guys. It's always all about the snow."

She tilted her head to the side, looking at him as if she wanted to say something else. Or maybe she wanted to protest. Before she could, Stevey Travor stopped goofing around on the snow and sauntered their way, a cocky grin on his face.

Portia changed the subject and because she seemed to be talking about something related to the exhibition, Cooper tried to focus on that instead of the need to charge headfirst into Stevey and beat the crap out of him.

"I was worried about transportation," Portia was saying. "It hadn't even occurred to me to think about where the exhibition was going to be and how to get the money types up here to see it."

"Hmm," he said noncommittally.

"I know!" she said. "I can't believe I didn't think about that. I've just been so busy working on the party Saturday night and arranging accommodations for everyone, I just didn't think about it. And—"

"And I told her that as long as we made sure we could get a snowplow up here, we could build the jump close to the road," Drew chimed in.

"Did you know they could do that?" she asked Cooper. "Just move the snow around and make a jump anywhere they want? How crazy is that?"

He arched an eyebrow. "You do remember that I'm a snowboarder, too, right?"

"Well, yeah, but—"

Just then Stevey reached them. "Hey, old man." He clapped Cooper on the shoulder and winked at Portia. Cooper wanted to break the guy's hand. "You can't blame her for being impressed. I mean, everything we do is golden, right, babe?"

Cooper felt a wave of irrational anger wash over him. He didn't just want to break Stevey's hand; he wanted to rip it off. He wanted to tear the guy limb from limb so that he never boarded again. And just for good measure, break the guy's nose in a couple of places to knock that pretty-boy sheen off his face.

And that was it right there—the moment Cooper knew he was in deep trouble. Hell, he'd nearly lost his cool and beat the crap out of an innocent—well, sort of innocent—guy who was basically his friend, even if he was a bit of a jerk. And it was all over a woman he was supposed to be done with by the time the weekend was over. Done.

Except he apparently wasn't done at all.

"Okay," he said, taking Portia by the shoulders and steering her over to his snowmobile. "I think it's time I get you back to the lodge. The flooring guys said they needed your input on something."

"Is it about the wax? Because I wasn't sure about that shade of brown and—"

"Yeah. Absolutely. Total wax nightmare."

She dug in her heels a few steps later. "Wait. Don't you want to watch them finish? It's really pretty impressive."

"Yeah, man," Stevey said with a cocky grin. "If you want to stay, I can take her back."

"No. It's fine. I know what you're capable of. It's nothing I haven't seen before."

"I don't understand," Portia said as she stared at the empty entrance hall of Bear Creek Lodge. The floor guys were nowhere to be seen. Their van wasn't even out in front. They'd left yellow caution tape strung across the door with a note saying no one could walk on the floors for at least twelve hours. More to the point, the wax job was clearly finished and looked amazing. She turned to Cooper. "What's going on?"

He took a step forward like he was going to walk right through the tape. She pushed a hand into his chest. "Oh, no, you don't, mister."

When she broke off suddenly, he raised his eyebrows in question.

Damn. Why had she touched him? His muscles were firm beneath her hand, despite the layers of clothes separating them. She couldn't think when he was near. She had to force a casual note into her voice. "Didn't you read the sign? No walking on the floor."

"So, what, we're just supposed to stand out here in the cold?"

She pointed down the porch. "No, we can go in through the back door to the kitchen if we need to, but let's not touch much there, either. The cleaning crew worked for four days to get it inspection-ready and the inspector is coming tomorrow."

Once she'd let them in the back door, she turned to him, frowning. "So what's the deal? You acted like there was some big emergency. What's wrong?"

"I just don't want you hanging out with Drew and Stevey and The Friends, that's all."

"Oh." She blew out a breath, unsure what she was supposed to do with this information. "So you don't want me around your friends."

"It's no big deal. It would just be best for everyone if you spent as little time with them as possible."

"I see." His words stung more than she wished they did, and she turned away from him so that he couldn't see the hurt in her eyes. They weren't together. Maybe they had seemed like a couple for the past few weeks, but they weren't. She'd momentarily forgotten the boundaries of their no-pressure fling. There was no need for her to be around his friends.

Maybe she was being too sensitive. Maybe this shouldn't hurt her, but it did.

She stared sightlessly at the kitchen. It wasn't much by the standards of a modern industrial kitchen, but it was one of her favorite rooms in the lodge. If you looked beyond the aging stainless-steel appliances, you could see the bones of the grand kitchen it had been when Wallace had first built Bear Creek Lodge. Thankfully, the Becks had only done the bare minimum of updates, leaving the solid maple cabinetry and massive butcher-block table in place. But like much of Bear Creek Lodge, you had to look beyond the surface to see the real beauty. Some people were no good at that. "Well, I guess that makes sense. Okay."

"Thank you," Cooper said gruffly.

But still it stung. And maybe she should have let it go. After all her years of marriage to Dalton, she was good at letting things go. But wasn't that the kind of thinking that had gotten her into trouble with her marriage in the first place? When she'd filed for divorce, hadn't she sworn that she was done just letting things slide? That she was going to fight for herself more often?

So why wasn't she standing up for herself now? Because she genuinely liked Cooper and she didn't want him to think she was a bitch?

She was so bad about that. In general, the more she liked someone, the more important they were to her, the less likely she was to show that person the real her. She was always so afraid of screwing up or doing the wrong thing or being an embarrassment. So she hid all her silliness, her propensity for panic attacks, her sensitivity. She buried it deep. But—as Cooper had pointed out—this wasn't long-term.

Besides, Cooper had seen beneath the polished facade long ago. He knew she had the heart of a flibbertigibbet. He knew she was overly sensitive and flighty and a little bit wack-a-doodle.

So there was no reason not to tell him exactly how she felt.

Even though Portia had said it was fine, when she turned back around to face him a moment later, he could see in her expression that it wasn't. Not at all. Her brow had furrowed and her eyes had darkened to match her tumultuous expression. Her lush, gorgeous lips twisted into a grimace.

"But you know, it's really not okay."

Uh-oh.

"It isn't?" he asked.

"No. It isn't. I was getting along fine with them. And, frankly, I'm a little annoyed that you even feel like you have to barge in and say anything."

"Oh, so I'm supposed to just stand there and say nothing while you hang out with Stevey freaking Travor?"

"Look, I get it. We're not really together and you don't want them thinking we are. Fine. You want me to stay away from your friends, and I'll do it. But it's kind of rotten, you know? Because they were genuinely nice to me and now I have to act like the bitch and be all cool and distant. I'll do it, but just so you know, I think you're a jerk for expecting me to."

She seemed to run out of steam then, because she just stood there, glaring at him. Her delicate skin had flushed a deep pink and her chest was rising and falling rapidly—as if she'd just run a mile. Or torn him a new one.

"You done?" he asked softly.

Her gaze narrowed, like she was thinking it over, trying to decide if she had anything else she wanted to throw at him. But then she nodded.

"First off—" he started walking toward her, slowly, because he was half-afraid she was so amped up she'd bolt if he moved too fast "—I'm not asking you to be a bitch. I don't care if you like them and want to be their friend. I don't even care if you want to start a frickin' book club with them."

Her frown deepened. "Then why were you so adamant about me not hanging out with them?"

Her complete and total confusion charmed him. She truly didn't see it. At all.

By now he'd closed the distance between them. She had backed herself into the corner of the kitchen. She still looked skittish, like she might want to run, but he reached out a hand and cupped her cheek.

"I don't want you hanging out with them because I'm trying to protect you."

"You're protecting me from them?"

"Stevey Travor is a womanizer. He'd talk your pants off you in a second if he had a chance."

She looked completely baffled, then she laughed. "You're worried I might sleep with Stevey Travor? That's absurd."

Her amusement did not improve his mood. "I've seen Stevey in action. He's quite charming."

"He's like a big puppy dog. And he's a decade younger than me. He's a child."

"Great," he groused. "I'm glad this amuses you."

She shook her head, a smile playing across her lips. "And I'm pretty sure it would never occur to him to seduce me. It's just silly."

"It's not silly. And it's driving me crazy."

"It's driving you crazy?" she asked, her voice sounding breathless.

"Yes." He stood a few inches away from her, taking in everything about her. He'd been away from her for over two weeks. It felt like a lifetime. Why was that? How was it that this woman—whom he'd known for years and had always been able to force out of his mind in the past—was suddenly someone he could hardly function without? He studied her, taking in everything from her adorable Heidi braids to her sun-kissed cheeks. She'd blossomed these past few weeks, but her appeal went far beyond her physical appearance.

"Should I apologize?" she asked sheepishly.

"I can't explain it. It doesn't make any sense, but the thought of you with any of those guys—hell, with any guy—it drives me crazy with jealousy."

Something that looked like sorrow flickered through her gaze. "I'm sorry, Cooper. I'm sorry it makes you uncomfortable. But it doesn't have anything to do with me."

"Are you kidding? It has everything to do with you."

Her face set into stubborn lines and she pushed her way past him. "No. It really doesn't. You said yourself that you don't want to be in a relationship. You have no interest in me outside the bedroom. Isn't that the point of a no-pressure fling? That means you don't get to be jealous. A husband would have the right to be jealous. A boyfriend would. But not you. All you ever wanted was to take me to bed. That's just about my body, so I don't see what that has to do with me at all."

"You think this is just about sex?"

"Do you think it's about anything else?"

"If it was your body I lusted after, I would have found a way to take you to bed years ago. I wouldn't have spent the past decade tormented by the idea that you were in love with and married to my brother. It's not just your body that I want. It's not thoughts of your body that keep me up at night. It's you. With all your quirks and funny little personality ticks. It's your pride and your stubbornness and your compassion. It's your sheer mule-headed determination to do the right thing no matter what. It's your very soul." He laughed then, because if he didn't know better, if he didn't know that love was a fantasy, he'd think that what he'd just described was a man in love.

Thirteen

Standing there, listening to Cooper talk about how much he wanted her, she knew there were a lot of reasons why she shouldn't be falling a little bit more in love with him with every word. But somehow she couldn't stop herself from hearing him. Couldn't stop herself from believing everything he said. In fact, all she could do was reach for him. Give herself what she most wanted. In that moment. Which was to rise up onto her toes and press her mouth to his.

That simple invitation was all that he needed. He met her move for move, tracing the seam of her lips with his tongue until she let him in. He tasted like mint and sweet spring water. He stroked her tongue with his in a way that made her tremble. Cooper kissed the same way he did everything—with confidence that bordered on arrogance, with skill that made her mind spin.

He was fearless in a way that took her breath away. As if he'd never had a single doubt about kissing her. As if he knew this was exactly what she wanted.

And it was.

This time, when he kissed and touched her, he lacked the finesse he'd had the previous times they'd made love. Instead of skill, he was all need. Instead of expertise, he was barely controlled desperation.

His hands moved down her back, pulling her to him until she was molded against him. Only her hands were between them, moving across his shirt, exploring the rock-hard muscles of his chest.

And then his hands skimmed down her side to squeeze her hips before slipping around to cup her bottom. Pleasure spiraled through her, and a low groan was torn from her throat.

"Damn, Portia," he muttered, his words nearly a groan, as well.

He lifted her up and against him, his mouth trailing a hot line of kisses down her neck. Each place his lips touched her skin lit a fire that spread through her body. She arched toward him. Then suddenly, she was off the ground. He'd lifted her clean off her feet onto the counter, and her legs automatically wrapped around his hips, pulling his hard length against her core. A shudder of raw pleasure coursed through her body. Somehow, he seemed to know exactly what she needed. Just how to touch her so that she came undone.

His kiss affected her in a way nothing else ever had. And maybe this was the last time she'd ever get to experience it. It was as though his very touch heated her blood and made her head spin. As though his kisses sucked the air right out of her lungs. She drew in quick, desperate breaths, but he only filled her senses more, the warm woodsy scent of him hitting her in the gut, making her greedy for him. She wanted him naked before her. She tugged at his shirt, pushing her hands under the fabric so that her palms could knead his bare skin.

And still that pressure inside her kept building until she was desperate. For all of him.

A moment later he was whipping her turtleneck up and over her head. The rest of her clothes followed so quickly she barely remembered them coming off. No man had ever seemed so eager to get her naked. And it felt good. Amazing to have him still wanting her like this. Cooper, who was like a rock star, who was so sought after that his assistant had to turn women away, who was handsome and accomplished and an amazing lover. And he wanted her. The experience was so heady, she didn't even protest as her clothing fell away.

For the briefest instant, she wondered if this was really her at all. The entire experience seemed beyond anything she'd ever done. Even anything she'd ever thought about doing.

But none of that seemed to matter, not when he was touching her. His fingertips trailing down her body, into her body, pushed all thoughts aside, burying who she really was so completely that when he slipped her panties down and knelt between her legs, she was beyond thought, let alone protest.

Because this woman, this woman sitting bare-assed naked on the counter while he devoured her, wasn't even her. That's what she told herself even when she shattered into tiny bits.

Cooper had meant to stop. Or at least to slow down. Or maybe just to ask and make sure that this was what she really wanted.

Instead, he'd lost himself in Portia's kiss. In her heated

response to his every touch. To her low moans and greedy mewling sounds. To the cool flutter of fingertips and the hot thundering of her heart. To the soft mounds of her ass and the damp folds of her sex. To her desperation. Her need. Her surprise.

At every step of the way, he told himself he was going to stop. Just one kiss, he'd said. Just one peek at her breasts. Just one nibble on her neck. Just one taste. Until he felt her coming apart against his tongue as tremor after tremor of her orgasm rocked through her body. That's when he stopped lying to himself.

He wasn't going to stop. Not until he'd driven her mad with pleasure at least a few more times tonight. Not until he'd felt the last of her defenses crumble as she'd climaxed while he was buried deep inside of her. Not until he'd erased every other man from her memory and her mind.

He carried her up the stairs to one of the empty bedrooms and then slowly made love to her. All the while forcing from his mind all the reasons they couldn't really be together. Not just the stupid, selfish reasons he'd always given to himself for not being in a real relationship, not that crap about not believing in love or happily ever afters. Those were the excuses he'd always given himself. The things that haunted him now were her reasons. All the reasons she didn't want to be with him. The fact that she'd been hurt too badly. That she wanted to adopt. That she couldn't see him as a father. That she couldn't imagine him in her life long-term.

And as long as he kept touching her, he was able to forget them.

He kissed his way back up her body, leaving a trail of pink where the day's growth of his beard scuffed her tender skin. Maybe he should have felt bad. Instead, he felt a deep surge of satisfaction at the sight. A sort of primitive pride that he didn't remember feeling with anyone else. He'd marked her as his. Not for forever, but for now. She was his.

He pinned her hands over her head and waited until she was looking him in the eye before he plunged into her. He needed her to see him. To acknowledge that he was the one making love to her. That he was the one who brought her pleasure over and over again. Making love to her was almost too much pleasure and in the end, he was the one who looked away. Because as much pleasure as he brought her, just being with her brought him more.

Portia awoke alone in the bedroom in Bear Creek Lodge that she'd been staying in whenever she worked too late to call the driver to take her back into town. After what had happened in the kitchen, Cooper had swept her up into his arms and carried her here to make love to her again. At some point after that, she'd slept, Cooper's body wrapped around hers, his hand clasping her breast possessively. Had she ever slept like that before? So closely entwined with someone else's body so that she felt it every time he moved? Had she ever felt that connected to a man?

She didn't think so.

She rolled over and buried her nose in the Cooper-scented pillow beside her and she was hit with another punch of that great scent. All pine-y and smoky. He smelled good. He always had.

He wasn't here, but that didn't surprise her. He'd probably gone out to see what Drew and The Friends were doing. He wouldn't want them to come looking for her and then to have to answer the inevitable questions any more than she did.

Still, lying there in bed, she had to admit this wasn't just sex. It was something so much more complicated than that. In the past few weeks, she'd grown to know Cooper. To understand how smart and driven he was. To respect him. To care deeply about him. What had started as a no-pressure fling had grown into something deep and complicated and nearly out of control.

But there was no room in her life for anything like that.

Things might have been different if he wanted a real relationship. She could have given herself over to the flame and let it burn her whole. But he didn't want that. He only wanted brief and shallow. He wanted sex without love.

At least that was what he'd said when they started this. She'd thought this afternoon that maybe he'd changed his mind. That maybe he felt more.

And when he'd carried her to the room and made such beautiful love to her, she'd been sure he'd been on the verge of saying so out loud.

Except, he hadn't. They'd had great sex and then he'd walked away.

She'd foolishly thought that she could let herself have this passionate fling, that as long as she knew going into it that it was just sex that she'd be safe. She'd been so wrong.

She was in way over her head. She wanted more. She needed more or nothing at all.

Settling for less than what she wanted seemed dirty and petty. It seemed small. It seemed disrespectful of her marriage.

Yes, her marriage to Dalton was over, but those ten years were still part of her life. It wasn't as if she could get them back or unwind them. She couldn't undo them. She wouldn't if she could. She certainly wouldn't turn her back on that part of herself. She had been so young and hopeful.

Portia respected that person too much to settle for something like this with Cooper.

She wouldn't settle for a cheap affair, but that didn't mean she was giving up, either. Somehow, inexplicably, she'd fallen in love with Cooper over the past three weeks.

She was dressed and heading down the servants' staircase in the back of the house when she heard the roar of snowmobiles outside the lodge. For just an instant, her hand gripped the railing. Was she ready for this? Ready to face the half-dozen rambunctious puppies as if nothing had happened?

Well, she supposed that was the good thing about puppies. Unless she met them on the porch wailing her heart out, they probably wouldn't notice. A few deep breaths later, she exited onto the porch via the kitchen door and followed the sounds of their raucous laughter.

Cooper was with them. In his snow gear, he blended seamlessly with the group as they parked their snowmobiles under a nearby copse of trees and started loading their equipment back into the waiting van. There was a lot of backslapping and boasting about who had done the most work and who had been a dumbass. For the first time, she felt a twinge of doubt about the coming days, not just about her relationship with Cooper, but also about whether or not this party of hers was a good idea at all. And about Cooper's idea for the lodge. He wanted to open an exclusive high-end lodge for snowboarders, but would snowboarders actually want to stay here?

Nothing about this group said exclusive or high-end. These guys didn't look as if they'd know luxury accommodations if they bit them on the nose.

Not for the first time, Portia felt a heartbreaking panic. She had doubts upon doubts. Fears on top of fears. Because in that moment she understood something about her relationship with Cooper. Yes, he wanted Bear Creek Lodge, but he wanted it for all the wrong reasons. He wanted prestige, the social acceptability that would come with owning a high-end resort. It wasn't the lodge he loved. It was the idea of the lodge. What owning the lodge would bring him.

Was his relationship with her just the same? Were they together because he wanted her, or because she represented success and wealth and privilege?

The idea made her sick to her stomach. But before she could flee back into the house, Stevey noticed her standing there and he nudged a couple of the other guys so they knew she was there, too. They settled down a bit. He bounded up the stairs to the porch.

"We finished! We'll be back tomorrow for test runs and to shoot some footage for the doc. You'll come watch, right?"

She glanced back down to see Cooper looking up at her, his expression unreadable. Then she smiled at Stevey, trying to hide her sorrow and confusion. "I don't know. I'll just have to see how things look here tomorrow."

"You should come," he insisted.

"I'll try," she agreed, but knew that *try* was the operative word there. She couldn't make any promises until she knew how things went with Cooper.

A moment later, Drew and The Friends all piled into the vans and headed back down the mountain.

Cooper came up onto the porch, propping his shoulder against one of the rough-hewn posts that held up the roof. "What were you talking to Stevey about?" he asked.

"He asked if I was going to come watch them practice tomorrow."

"What did you say?" he asked as he followed her in through the back door to the kitchen.

"I told him I'd have to wait and see." She sucked in an icy, bracing breath and plunged into the conversation she knew he wouldn't want to have. "I don't think this is a good idea. But Cooper, you and I need to talk."

Fourteen

He gazed at her through narrowed eyes, like he was just waiting to be sucker punched.

"I hired a P.I.," she said without ceremony.

She had wanted this conversation to go very differently. She had wanted to tell him after the exhibition as sort of a celebration. But then she'd met the snowboarders and now she had doubts about the lodge. Suddenly, she knew she had to tell him this now, while there was still a chance he'd listen.

"A P.I.?"

"His name is Jack Harding. I know Hollister said it was 'against the rules.'" She added air quotes in case he couldn't read her low opinion of Hollister's rules from just her tone. "But the way I see it, those rules are for you, Dalton and Griffin. I'm not competing for the money. I'm not technically in the game. So I figure I'm exempt. Which means I can hire anyone I want to find the heiress."

Cooper had crossed his arms over his chest and was watching her with an inscrutable expression.

She crossed to the kitchen counter, grabbed her tote bag and pulled out the few pages of emails from Jack that she'd printed out at the hotel business center. "I had him start looking for Ginger at the hotel where we held the Children's Hope Foundation gala." She flipped through the papers. "They had no idea who Ginger was, which seemed odd at first. But then the catering manager admitted that it wasn't unusual for them to hire temp waitstaff for events like that." She held out one of the papers to Cooper. "Here's the email from the temp agency. They don't have an employee named Ginger, either. Which made me think she must have given me a false name."

She paused, half expecting him to ask why Ginger would have done that. Portia looked at him expectantly, but he said nothing. Instead, he just stared at the page in front of him almost as if he wasn't even seeing it.

Then she continued, trying to recapture her previous interest in the search, but floundering a bit. When she and Jack had discussed all this, it had seemed like such a revelation. It had seemed important. "After all, when I talked with her, she'd just tipped a drink down my mother's back. She probably thought she was in trouble with her boss. So I asked Jack to go to the hotel and ask the other employees, which he did. And here's where it gets weird."

She paused again. This time, Cooper looked up at her, eyebrows raised infinitesimally.

"He talked to twenty-one employees and twelve of them remember a waitress matching her description, but no one remembers hiring her. Or paying her. And of those twelve employees, five of them remember different names. She's a phantom."

Cooper pushed the printouts back across the table toward

her, some of the tension in his expression fading. "I don't see what this has to do with anything. You found nothing."

She pushed the papers back defiantly. "This isn't nothing!"

"You didn't find her."

"No. I didn't find her real identity, but I definitely found her."

He tapped a finger in the center of the top page. "There's nothing here to indicate this is the woman at all."

"I found a woman who is trying very hard to hide her identity from us."

"Why on earth would she do that?"

"I think she knows we're looking for her. I think she knows she's Hollister's daughter." She was sure she was right. So sure about it that her heart was racing, slamming into her ribcage. "Everyone in Houston knows the Cains attend the Children's Hope gala. If she found out she was a Cain and just wanted to scope out the situation, that would be the perfect opportunity. She could walk in disguised as one of the waitstaff and watch the family members and see how they interact, all without revealing her identity to us."

"Your logic there is faulty," he said with a sneer. "You assume she's trying to hide her identity from *us.* When in fact, she may have no idea we exist. All we know for sure is that she's trying to hide her identity."

"What other reason could she have for showing up at the gala and working without getting paid?"

"She could be a pickpocket or a thief."

"Right. Your long-lost sister is a character in a Dickens novel." Why didn't he see it? Why was he so damn determined to make this complicated? "Or we could figure that maybe since the Cains have been searching for her for over a year that maybe somebody did something to tip their hand." She waited, heart still pounding, for some glimmer of interest from him. "Why are you so determined to downplay this? This is a clue about the identity of your sister."

He whirled on her. "No, it's not. You haven't discovered anything about her. This is just more information about a woman we're not even sure exists. What is it you expect me to feel here?"

She threw up her hands. "I don't know. I don't even care. I just want you to feel something."

"Why?" He stalked a step closer to her. "Why should I feel anything about this? Even if you actually found Hollister's daughter, even if she was standing right outside the door, why should I feel anything about her?"

"Because she's your sister."

"No. She's not. I don't have a sister. This woman, whoever she is, is just another one of Hollister's bastards. For all we know, there are dozens of women just like her. Hell, there are probably hundreds. So why the hell are we all so hot to find this one woman?"

"Because she's your sister," Portia repeated, softly this time, because she almost couldn't speak past the lump of emotion clogging her throat.

"I have nothing in common with this woman. Shared genetic code does not make her my family."

"Is that how you feel about Griffin and Dalton, too?"

"Yes."

"Even though you spent summers with them since you were ten."

"Yes."

"Even though you lived with them after your mom died? Even though Caro took you in?"

"The fact that I lived in the same house with them never made me part of the family."

Her frustration burst out. "You know what, you're right. It didn't." Now it was her turn to stalk closer to him. "You know what makes someone part of the family? Spending time with them. If you'd wanted to be part of the Cain family, then you damn well should have made an effort. For years, I invited you to visit. I invited you for Thanksgiving and Christmas. Every time we had any kind of family gathering, I invited you. You almost never showed up. Half the time you didn't even bother to reply, so don't bitch now about not being part of the family."

He tipped his head back and laughed. "That's great. Just great."

She blinked, startled by his mercurial mood shift. "What?"

"You. Giving me a hard time about not coming to family functions."

"Why is that funny?" He was still laughing and it unnerved her. What didn't she know?

"It's not funny so much as ironic." The laughter settled into a grin tinged with bitterness. "You ever think about why I didn't attend all those warm family gatherings?"

"You were busy. You had work and travel." She parroted the excuse he'd always given her. And then, so she wasn't the only one thrown off-balance, she added, "And I assume plenty of Swedish models to keep you occupied."

"Right. The Swedish models. Haven't you ever wondered why all those Swedish models bother you so much?"

He was clearly baiting her, so she bumped her chin up and narrowed her gaze. "As a feminist I don't like to see any woman devalue herself so much that she'll sleep with a guy merely because he has an Olympic medal."

He smirked. "Nice try, but no. The Swedish models bother you for the same reason I never came to Cain holiday functions."

She frowned. "There's no connection—"

"I stayed away all those years because I knew I was attracted to you. I stayed away because I knew you felt it, too."

She wanted to protest, but all her words were encased in shock. And he didn't give her a chance to say anything anyway.

He closed the distance between them in a few quick steps and cupped her jaw in his hands. His touch was gentle, but firm, unrelenting, so that she had no choice but to meet his gaze.

"There's been an attraction between us since that day in the church. I've wanted you. I stayed away because it was easier than being around seeing you married to my brother."

She shook her head. "I would never have—"

"I know that. You're a good person, maybe the best person I know. Decent in a way that Dalton didn't even deserve. And I know you never would have acted on that attraction. But that wouldn't have stopped me from being the jerk who tried to tempt you. So I stayed away."

She just stood there, staring into his amazing blue eyes, watching the emotions flicker in his gaze. A horrible pain spread through her chest, crushing her lungs, breaking her heart.

Because until now, she hadn't been ready to face the real reason they couldn't be together—her relationship with Dalton. Sure, they'd talked about Dalton and about her marriage, but neither of them had gone so far as to admit that this attraction had been simmering for years.

As long as this was just a fling, it didn't matter. It was just between the two of them and neither of them had to face the reality of what a relationship would mean.

"You're right," she said numbly.

"I am."

"I mean, yes, there always has been something between us. Neither of us ever would have acted on it, but it was there. And as long as this was just a mindless fling, I could pretend that none of this—what's happening now—had any connection to my real life. But I don't think I can pretend that anymore."

He just stared at her blankly. "So then we're over," he finally said.

His words made her heart break a little more, even though she had no idea why, because their relationship had always had a sell-by date. They were never going to last forever, so why did it hurt so much to end it?

"Yes."

He strode over to her and grabbed her arms, pulling her toward him just a little, searching her expression. "I'm not okay with this."

"I'm not, either," she admitted. "But what's the alternative? That we start dating? That I take you home to meet my parents? That we tell your brother that we're sleeping together? For what? All because we happen to enjoy each other's company in bed? Look, I know that's not how this works. Women are like accessories to you. The naughty models and Olympic scandal were for the rebellious stage of your life. But now that you want respectability, you're going for the nice rich girl and the high-end hotel. This has been fun, but I never expected it to last forever."

She purposely threw his words back at him. It was petty of her, the way she wanted to hurt him just a little bit because he'd hurt her so much, but she did it anyway.

He dropped her arms and stepped back. "No. I guess neither of us wants that." He shook his head, letting out a bitter little laugh. "But I'm still not okay with it."

"Well, if you don't like that, then you're really not going to like this. I don't think this is a good idea."

"You and I?" he asked grimly. "I think we just covered this territory."

"Not you and I. This. Turning Bear Creek Lodge into a luxury resort."

His gaze narrowed. "You've gotten too attached to it, haven't you? You got caught up in the romanticism of the history and—"

"That's not it." He started to say something else, but she held up her hands to cut him off. "Stop interrupting me and let me get this out. It's not that I don't want you messing up the lodge. It's that I think anything you do to this place is getting in your own way."

"That doesn't even make sense."

"Yes, it does. You're so sure that there's a market for a high-end resort for snowboarders, and I'm sure you're right. But would you actually want to hang out with the snowboarder who would come here? I've met your friends. They would come here because you're here, but they wouldn't come here just for the resort."

"You think Drew and Stevey and those guys are my friends?"

"They came here to help you, didn't they?"

"They came here for the snow."

"No. They came here for you. Because they think you're great. You weren't out there when they were building the jump. You didn't hear the things they said about you. I know you think they were just hitting on me, but you're wrong. It never even crossed their minds, because they all assumed we were together. They all talked you up to me. They may enjoy the powder, but they came here for you. Because you're their friend."

For a second, he just stared at her, like he couldn't quite wrap his brain around her words. Then his gaze dropped and he gave a little nod. "Maybe."

"And if I had to guess, I'd say you genuinely like them,

too. That you admire them more than you do some jerk like Robertson or your father."

His lips twisted into a smile. "That's obvious."

"So then why are you so desperate to prove yourself to Robertson and Hollister? Why do you give a damn what they think? Why not do whatever the hell you want to with this lodge? Why not market it to people whose opinion matters to you?"

When he looked back up at her, his expression was flat. "I'm marketing it to people like you."

She felt a stab of pain near her heart. "Exactly. You're marketing to people like me."

People who he thought cared about luxury and style more than substance.

"Don't you get it?" she asked. "You're marketing this hotel to people you don't really like. People you wouldn't want to spend time with. I think it's a mistake."

He just looked at her. "After all this work we've both put into this, now you're telling me? What's the point?"

"The point is, I'm not going to be around to tell you these things next week or the week after. If I think you're making a mistake, I have to tell you now. Now is all I have."

That had seemed so simple just a few weeks ago. But in this moment, it broke her heart to admit it aloud.

She waited to see if he would acknowledge her words, if he would admit that she was right. But instead, he just shook his head.

"You're wrong. Beck's Lodge is going to be amazing. It's the best thing I can do with Flight+Risk."

She wanted to keep arguing with him, but what else could she say? In the end, it was his decision. Maybe Bear Creek Lodge would be his downfall after all. It had certainly been hers.

Fifteen

Until she saw the resort through Cooper's eyes, she hadn't realized how much she had accomplished. It about killed her, because she still knew that this was a mistake; there was just nothing she could do to convince Cooper of it. Still, if she blocked out how miserable this was going to eventually make him, if she pretended this was just a business move and not deeply personal, then she could appreciate the amazing changes in Bear Creek Lodge.

The only renovations they'd done to the building itself were to demolish the ancient registration desk and pull up the carpet to restore the original hardwood floors.

All the other changes were staging. She'd moved out the aging lobby furniture and replaced it with only a few clusters of chairs. A small stage had been set up in the corner for the band she'd hired. Buffet tables had been set up where the registration desk had once been. The rest was lighting, lighting, lighting. It was amazing how you could manipulate the beauty of a room by highlighting its best features and casting its bad ones in shadow. Portia took comfort knowing that when the guests arrived this evening for the exhibition kickoff, they would have to look very closely to see the toll that the past sixty years had taken on the once-glorious lodge. It was small comfort, but she took it where she could get it.

In fact, things appeared perfect as Portia strolled around the room, surveying everything. The guests would start arriving in the next thirty minutes. The caterers was already putting out appetizers. The band—a popular cover band from Provo—was already set up in the corner.

Cooper walked up to her, stopping to survey the room. He stood close, but pointedly didn't touch her. There was space between them that hadn't been there before. An immeasurable gulf of misunderstandings and cross-purposes.

Part of her yearned for his touch—nothing romantic or sexual—just something comforting. But he didn't reach for her and she didn't budge in his direction, either. She'd dressed in a pair of navy palazzo pants and a flowing top with just a little bit of shimmer to it. Her hair was swept up into a relaxed twist. She hoped that she looked cool and wealthy. Like the perfect hostess for this event, even if she didn't feel like it on the inside.

"Everything looks just right," he said, his tone cold. "I knew you could pull it off."

She turned to look at him. "We haven't pulled it off yet. We still have the rest of the evening to get through and tomorrow. And that's just the beginning, right? After that, we have to see if you've convinced any investors that this is a safe bet. Or if you can sway the board. There are still a lot of ifs in play."

Cooper looked around the room, his gaze taking on a possessive glint. "No. There aren't. This place looks amazing. No one who comes here is going to have any doubts that this is meant to be."

Her stomach soured and she knew he was right. He was so determined—so focused—it was impossible to believe that he wouldn't succeed. Even though this was the last thing he needed.

The party was in full swing a few hours later when Cooper looked up from talking to one of the investor types to see the last man he would have expected walking through the front doors—his brother Dalton. Laney was on his arm. Dalton paused just inside the door to help her out of her coat, which he handed to the attendant. Laney looked lovely in a vibrant yellow dress. Once her coat was off, they both stepped aside to reveal Griffin and his wife, Sydney, right behind them.

Jesus. It was like a Cain family reunion.

Who the hell had invited them?

Before the thought could even settle in his mind, Portia crossed to their side. She gave Laney and Sydney hugs and brief air kisses. And then Dalton gave her a real hug. Somehow the sight of that made Cooper's gut twist with jealousy. Not the superficial jealousy that he'd felt about Drew and Stevey, but something deep and dark. Something rooted in a lifetime of resentment.

By the time he reached them, Portia was shaking Griffin's hand with a friendly smile.

"Dalton. Griffin." Cooper nodded. "I didn't realize you'd been invited."

"I invited them," Portia said smoothly.

"You did?" Cooper turned to look at Portia, who smiled back innocently.

"Yes. Did you know, Cooper, that Sydney's youngest brother has an interest in snowboarding?"

"I did not know that," he said through a tight smile.

"Trust me, it's not something I encourage." Sydney laughed. "But we all wanted to see what you've been up to." To Portia she added, "After all the praise you heaped on this place, we're hoping it was a real showstopper."

"And what do you think?" Portia asked with a smile.

"It's amazing," Laney said. "I can see why you're so enthusiastic."

He shot Portia a look, trying to read her expression. Had she invited Dalton and Laney before or after she'd decided this whole project was a crappy idea? Had she invited them to support him or prove a point?

The band was playing a song from the sixties. The kind of classic anyone would love to get up and dance to, and the crowd was eating it up.

"You should go dance," Portia said. She pulled out her phone, where she somehow had the queue of songs listed. "The next song is a jazz ballad. It'll be perfect. After that, I can fill you in on the fascinating history of the building and tell you all about Cooper's plans."

Right on cue, the band drifted from the dance classic to a sultry jazz standard.

Portia smiled at him as if she hadn't just fed him to the wolves. "Perhaps you'd ask me to dance, Cooper?"

He wanted to tip his head back and howl with frustration. He wanted to storm out, find a board somewhere and get lost in the icy snow. To walk away from her and everything she represented, everything he couldn't have. Because he couldn't have her, no matter how much he wanted her. Instead, he took her arm and led her out onto the dance floor, relishing the feel of her body against his even as his anger threatened to boil over. But he tamped that all down, and grasped her hand in his. He let his fingers rest at the small of her back, just where her blouse hung loose, so that his fingertips grazed her bare skin.

"That was a nice trick," he said. "You invite them here just to prove a point?"

She met his gaze coolly. "Yes, but probably not the point you think."

"Okay, I'll bite. What point are you trying to make? That I don't have what it takes to open this hotel? That in the end, I'll always be outclassed by Dalton and Griffin?"

"See? I knew you were going to misinterpret things." Despite her chiding words, she smiled up at him. There was something sad and heartbreaking about her smile. "I invited them here because you hadn't seen them in years."

"Thanks to Hollister's stupid quest and their weddings, I've seen more of them in the past year than I ever have."

"I hardly think meeting against the backdrop of Hollister's ridiculous challenge counts as fertile ground for a healthy brotherly relationship."

"That's assuming I want that kind of relationship."

She stopped dancing. They were in the middle of the dance floor, and other couples moved around them seamlessly in time to the music. "I think you've spent so much of your life resenting them just because they're Hollister's sons that you no longer know what you want, let alone what you need." She continued to meet his gaze unflinchingly. "You need friends that appreciate you for who you are. You need a family that loves you. The thing is, you already have those things. They're right there. You just refuse to acknowledge them."

"And this seemed like a great idea? To drop this on me right now?"

She tipped her head slightly to the side. "No. Not at all. But when else do I have? You and I are over after this weekend. This is my last chance."

"You think you know exactly what I need? Just like you think you know what I should do with Beck's Lodge?"

"No. I don't care what you do with this place. I love this building, but I only care about what you need. Make it into a hotel or don't. But you know what I think you do need? You need more people in your life who care about you. Either way, I don't want to be your excuse for not having a relationship with your family."

"I don't need a relationship with them."

"Yes. You do. Everybody needs family. And you're the one who told me you've stayed away from yours for years because of me. I'm not okay with that. I don't want to stand between you and your brothers."

He dropped his hands from her body. "So. That's what this is about?"

"Your relationship with the Cains? That's what this has been about for a while now."

"No. That's not what I meant." A few of the other couples had noticed that they weren't dancing, so he stepped closer to her and pulled her back into his arms. This time, he felt only cold anger as he held her. "You just can't resist fixing people, can you?"

She frowned, looking off-balance for the first time tonight. "I don't…I don't know what you mean."

"You think I want to be another one of your charity projects? Like the heiress you're so determined to protect? Like Caro? Like those foster kids you plan to adopt?"

"I don't… That's not what this is."

"Are you sure?" Doubt flickered through her gaze and just like that his anger dissolved into something softer but no less painful. How could he still be angry with her? "You are so damn sensitive. You care so much about other people. You can't help it. But I am not another fixer-upper. I will not be an object of pity for you."

He dropped his hands from her body and this time he walked away. He was done dancing.

She must have been done, as well, because at the end of the night, when the last busload of guests went back down the mountain to the hotel in Provo, she went with them. And she didn't come back the next day.

Sixteen

Cooper had consumed her life for those brief weeks she'd been at Bear Creek Lodge.

The whole time she'd been there, part of her had been convinced they were going to fail. That Bear Creek Lodge would be Cooper's folly. It had never occurred to her that it would be her own.

And yet the exhibition had been a huge success. She had seen that even though she'd left partway through. The lodge had looked amazing. The guests had had a fabulous time. More importantly, the guests who were also investors had been impressed.

She had left Utah with no doubt at all that Cooper would be able to purchase, renovate and open Bear Creek Lodge. Either his own board would support the decision and the resort would open under the Flight+Risk name or other investors would step forward. She wouldn't be surprised if he'd already received numerous offers. Offers she would never know anything about.

She still didn't believe opening the lodge would make him happy, but what could she do? She'd tried her best to give him an opening to repair his relationship with his brothers. She couldn't do any more than that—other than hope.

Before leaving Bear Creek Lodge, she'd cleared out the little room she'd stayed in occasionally—the room she and Cooper had made love in. She'd headed back into Provo for the night and taken the first flight out in the morning. She hadn't even waited for the first flight to Texas, but instead had just headed east. Between long flights and rushed connections, it took her almost eighteen hours to get back to her cozy house near the Galleria. It felt like years had passed since she'd been there.

She didn't even give herself a chance to settle in but immediately called Jack Harding for the latest update on the missing heiress. Then she printed up all the information in the file and delivered it to Caro. Caro might be too proud to tell her sons about the state of her finances. She might be too proud to ask for help from anyone. But it had occurred to Portia that if Caro found the heiress on her own and presented the information to Dalton and Griffin, then they would almost definitely split the money with her. It was the simplest and easiest solution.

And Portia felt like an idiot for not thinking of it sooner. Instead, she'd come up with a solution that had complicated everyone's lives.

After that, like a bear going to ground for winter, she hunkered down, living like a shut-in for a week, talking on the phone only to her mother, who was baffled by her behavior.

Of course her mother—being a supreme gossip hound—had heard all about the exhibition and Portia's part in it.

There were phone calls—lots of them—from her mother. Fretful ones. Anxious ones. Critical ones.

It took a week for Celeste to run out of things to say. Portia knew Celeste could have held out a lot longer if Portia had given her anything to work with. But Portia refused to comment or defend herself, so eventually Celeste ran out of steam and left Portia alone. After that, Celeste had just ordered Portia to get herself together in time for the next gala on the society schedule.

It wasn't until two days later when her doorbell rang that she decided she'd had enough. For once in her life, her mother just needed to bug off.

Except it wasn't her mother at the door. It was Laney.

Portia just stood there in her yoga pants and Scooby Doo T-shirt, gaping at the sight of the woman on her doorstep. Laney's pregnancy was just beginning to show and she had an adorable little bump tenting her vintage dress, a bump that her gorgeous gown from the other night had hidden. Her hair looked thick and glossy. Her cheeks glowed. She did not look like she'd spent the past week watching Nicholas Sparks movies and eating Pizza Rolls. And an entire Sara Lee pound cake.

Unfortunately, Portia was pretty sure that's exactly what she looked like.

Laney seemed not to notice. Instead, she threw her arms around Portia and gave her a rib-crunching hug. The bag Laney was holding swung around and bumped Portia's hip.

"Okay, I know it's weird, me coming over," she said as she pulled back. "But your mom called Dalton and asked him to come talk to you. He said that was a sure sign things were bad and that he really should come. But I thought him coming would be even weirder. Besides, he clearly didn't even know what to say and he wasn't going to bring ice cream. Or any kinds of snacks. At all. Men."

Brushing past Portia, she held up the bag and gave it a jiggle. "I didn't know if you were a sweet snacker or a savory snacker, so I brought some of each." She plopped down on the sofa and started putting things out on the coffee table. "We have chips, guac, salsa, wasabi nuts, chocolate-covered almonds and five different flavors of Ben & Jerry's. What's your poison?"

Portia could only stare in amazement as Laney made herself at home. Laney.

Laney Cain was in her house. Her ex-husband's current wife had to visit. Apparently to make sure Portia was prepped for the zombie apocalypse.

That was bizarre, right?

"What are you doing here?" she asked stupidly.

Laney looked up, her cheeks flushing. "Look, I know it's weird." She looked down at the table and nudged the various jars of things so that they all lined up perfectly. "Everyone is really worried about you. When we saw you in Provo, we thought something was up between you and Cooper. We thought maybe something—" she gave an awkward shrug and tried to smile "—good. Dalton thought it was weird at first, but he got used to the idea. We were hopeful. Except you came back here early and Cooper's completely incommunicado, which just made us think maybe we should be worried. No one wanted to tell Caro because Hollister took a turn for the worse the other day and she's busy with that."

"Everyone's worried about me?"

"Yes! Sydney offered to come by instead of me, but she and Griffin are leaving the country tomorrow morning. But if you need them, they'll postpone the trip." She gave a little shrug. "Look, I know you probably don't like me. I can't blame you. And you don't even have to talk to me. You can just take my food and show me to the door. But if you want a friendly ear and a shoulder to cry on, you've got it. Besides, we're family, so you know whatever you tell me isn't going any further."

What could she say to that?

No, she didn't like Laney. She was the love of Dalton's life. Of course, Portia didn't like her.

Still, she was floored by the idea that Laney considered her family—let alone that she would go to all this effort on her behalf. The fact that Griffin and Sydney were talking about canceling their trip—for her—was baffling. Yes, she still had a good relationship with Caro, but she'd figured she was persona non grata with the rest of the Cains.

She walked over to the table and picked up the five pints of ice cream. "These will melt if we leave them out too long."

She headed off into the kitchen, wanting to steal a moment alone. She shoved the ice cream in the freezer and then stood there for several long heartbeats, her forehead pressed to the front of it. Mostly just feeling sorry for herself.

Then Laney said, from the doorway, "Dalton said you were too smart to let a guy like Cooper break your heart, but me…I know smart has nothing to do with it."

Part of her wanted to yell at Laney. Or have a temper tantrum. Or maybe just throw up her hands and cry.

She whirled around to face Laney. "Look, I appreciate the gesture. Thank you for coming and trying to help or whatever, but it's just too weird, okay? I'm not going to cry on your shoulder. There's not enough Ben & Jerry's in the world for that."

Laney just stared at her, an expression of sympathy on her face. Then she said softly, "You take care of a lot of people. Would it kill you to let someone take care of you for a change?"

Portia tilted her head to the side and just looked at Laney, trying to see past the layers of complication that separated them. She tried to imagine opening up to this woman, spilling her guts, crying her eyes out, eating Phish Food straight out of the container.

But she just couldn't see it.

So instead of bursting into tears and throwing herself into Laney's waiting arms, she answered the question that still hung in the air. "Yes. I think today it would kill me to let you take care of me. I can handle a lot, but I can't handle pity from you."

Laney looked like the protest she wanted to make was clawing its way out of her throat. But finally, she nodded, slowly crying the tears Portia wouldn't let herself shed. "Would it be better if it was one of the other Cains?"

Portia shook her head. There was only one Cain she wanted to see.

"Okay. I'll go," Laney said. But at the door she stopped and added, "You're wrong, though. It's not pity that brought me here. I know what it's like to be alone. To feel like you have no family. Not wanting you to feel like that isn't pity."

Laney left then, without giving Portia a chance to reply. She waited until she heard Laney's car drive off before she let the tears fall.

Cooper didn't know what to do with himself the next week, despite the fact that the rest of the weekend went off without a hitch. If Portia's quick departure could be considered without a hitch. Portia had planned everything so well that things ran smoothly without her. The guests were impressed. The snowboarders had a great time. The media ohhed and ahhed. By the following week, several investors had already approached him about buying in. By the week after that, his board, Robertson included, was clamoring to move forward and commit Flight+Risk to the project.

And none of it mattered.

He felt none of the joy or satisfaction he should have felt at his success.

In fact, he felt nothing at all, until he came home to his loft in Denver one night to find Dalton waiting on his doorstep. Even then, it was only mild surprise.

"Hey," he said with a nod as he opened the door.

Dalton waited until they'd entered the condo, then asked, "Did you sleep with Portia?"

Cooper didn't answer, but Dalton must have seen the truth in his face, because he hauled off and straight up punched him.

Cooper staggered back a step in surprise. "What the hell?"

He didn't have a chance to recover though because Dalton slammed into him again, this time shoulder first into his chest, plowing him back several steps until they both went feet over ass over the arm of the sofa.

"What the hell?" he asked again.

Still Dalton threw another punch. At that point, Cooper was just done. He caught Dalton with a jab to the kidneys. Dalton grunted and tried to dodge the blow. Cooper rolled on top of his brother and landed one more solid punch in Dalton's stomach before scrambling back. "I don't want to hurt you."

Dalton pushed himself up, the rage on his face dimming somewhat. "Yeah, well, I still want to hurt you."

"Why?" Cooper asked.

"Portia," Dalton answered, panting and rubbing his hand across his kidneys. "Because you screwed with Portia."

"Oh." Shock rocked him back on his heels. It took him a few seconds to process what his brother was saying. Then he pushed himself to his feet and stood, holding out his hand to Dalton. As he pulled Dalton up, he asked, "You want to hit me some more?"

"Yeah. I do." He rubbed his hand down his cheek and flexed his jaw. "But I think I'll give it a rest."

Cooper nodded and headed for his refrigerator. He pulled out two Sierra Nevadas, popped them both open and handed one to Dalton. "She's not yours."

Dalton glared at him before taking a long draw from the beer. "You think I don't know that? Of course she's not mine." He muttered something under his breath that sounded like *dumbass*. "But who the hell else does she have to come kick the ass of the guy who broke her heart?"

Cooper froze, the beer not quite to this mouth. That statement gave him pause for several reasons. First off, apparently he'd broken her heart. He'd known he'd hurt her. He'd known he'd pissed her off. He had not known he'd broken her heart. Secondly, apparently she'd shared this news with Dalton. Which surprised the hell out of him. But to Dalton, he merely said, "No one kicked your ass when you broke her heart."

"Someone should have."

Cooper raised his beer slightly in toast. "You wanna have another go? I'll do it right now."

Dalton ignored the jab and said, "Portia is an only child. Her parents are selfish nightmares. She's essentially alone in the world. You wouldn't know it to look at her, but she doesn't make friends easily." He took a drag of beer. "I did a lot of things wrong when I was with her, but I always treated her with respect. And I have a hell of a lot of admiration for her. She deserves better than to be jerked around by someone like you."

"Yeah. I couldn't agree more." The words were out of his mouth before he even knew he was saying them. "She does deserve better. If I thought for a second that she really did love me, then things would be different."

Dalton eyed him for a long moment. "So you're just

going to leave it at that? You're just going to let her go? You're not even going to try to fight for her? Because you never struck me as the kind of guy who would back down from a fight."

"I'm not."

Finally, Dalton shook his head, a smile pulling at his lips. "Then what the hell are you doing here? If you want to be with her, then you should be in Houston, begging her to take you back."

Seventeen

Having Laney come to her house was just what Portia needed to pull herself out of her funk. There were a lot of things Portia could put up with, but being pitied by Laney was not one of them. She was done moping around.

Still, it was hard to get back to her normal routine when she didn't really have a normal routine. Much of her life was defined by the fund-raising schedule for Children's Hope Foundation and the other organizations she worked with, but this was a particularly slow time of year for her. However, she did follow up and make an appointment with a social worker she knew. The process of adopting through the foster system was totally different than the private adoption she'd been pursuing with the adoption lawyer. She was starting over. If she was going to adopt then she had a lot of paperwork to get started on. There were classes to take and applications to fill out. She had enough to keep her so busy she wouldn't have time to think about Cooper. Almost.

She was just returning from her appointment when she noticed an unusual car parked in front of her house. But then she saw it was a sporty model with a rental agency sticker on the back and she only knew one guy who rented a sports car every time he came to Houston. Her foot hesitated on the accelerator as she pulled into the driveway, tempted, if only briefly, to drive right on past and ignore Cooper's presence.

But that would be cowardly, and Cooper wasn't the kind of man who would take being put off forever.

He was sitting on her doorstep, waiting, and he stood when she climbed out of the car.

He was dressed in jeans and a navy Henley that made the blue in his eyes seem deeper and more mysterious. His expression was dark and heated as he looked at her. He held a leather-bound book in his hands. The very sight of him made her heart race and her knees weak. How could she be this close to him and not just throw herself in his arms? Why was he here? What could he possibly want?

Despite her endless questions, she didn't say anything, but just unlocked the door to let him in.

"We had a deal," he said as she shut the door behind them.

It took her a second to realize what he was talking about. "We did. I held up my end of it."

He nodded, holding the book out to her. "You never gave me a chance to hold up my end of the bargain. I'm supposed to help you find the heiress."

She looked at him suspiciously. "What's this?"

"It's my mother's journal."

"And how is this supposed to help me?"

He ducked his head for a second, scrubbing his palm over his hair before meeting her gaze again. "Just look at it, okay?"

She flipped open the book and thumbed through the pages. There were handwritten pages interspersed with newspaper clippings. All articles about Hollister or Cain Enterprises.

"I don't understand," she said.

"When I was a kid, my mother was obsessed with Hollister. She was convinced that their brief fling was true love. That he was going to divorce Caro and marry her. She read and collected everything about him. She got the Houston newspapers for years so that she could clip the articles. This book is all the information she had about him. It's from about the time when he probably had the affair with the heiress's mother. I don't know if there's anything in there or not. Maybe there's some clue about what Hollister was up to. It might help."

Portia stared at the pages in front of her, unable to stop looking. Without taking her eyes from the book, she backed up to the sofa and slowly sat down. The journal was detailed. Exhaustive. As Cooper had said, obsessive.

Cooper had brought it to her because it might have information about Hollister's life, but she couldn't help thinking about the glimpse into Cooper's life it provided. What had it been like to grow up with a mother like this? How had it shaped Cooper's view of the Cains? Of the world?

Almost as if he had read her mind, he said, "I don't want you to think she was crazy."

She glanced up, her heart breaking a little at the protective glint in his gaze. No matter what else he thought about his mother, he had loved her. He still did.

"I don't think that," she said.

"They had met when she was skiing in Europe. She was a model. It was her first international photo shoot. She got pregnant. Her modeling career was over. Her parents hadn't wanted her to go into modeling and refused to take her back in when they found out she was going to have a baby. She didn't have a lot of options."

"But Hollister supported her, right?"

"Yeah. She didn't have any education. She didn't make good choices with the money. She paid for skiing lessons and vacations in Vale, but we lived in crap apartments." He let out a laugh that was sad and bitter and lonely. It was the laugh of countless disappointed hopes. Of crushed paternal affection. "She wanted us to be ready for the good life when Hollister came back and married her."

Portia carefully closed the book and set it on the coffee table before standing. She wanted more than anything to pull him into her arms. To stroke his back. To comfort the child he'd been. To protect that boy from the heartless cruelty Hollister had undoubtedly bestowed.

She knew what a bastard Hollister was. Yes, he'd been charming and handsome and charismatic when he wanted to be. But all that covered a ruthless ambition and a lack of concern for others that bordered on sociopathic.

When she thought of Cooper as a child—hopeful, energetic, eager—coming face-to-face with his own father's apathy...well, when she thought of that, she wanted to drive across town and drive a stake through Hollister's heart, because surely monsters like him could only be killed that way.

However, she didn't pull Cooper into her arms, because she knew if their positions had been reversed, if it had been her revealing that information, she wouldn't have wanted comfort. Wasn't she the one just the other day who'd told Laney to leave because she couldn't stand her pity? Wasn't she the one who—

Ah, screw it.

She threw herself at him, and he caught her. She held

on tight, trying to squeeze a lifetime of love into that one embrace.

For the first time, there was nothing sexual about his embrace. It was just comforting.

After a moment, he whispered, “I didn’t come here for your pity.”

“This isn’t pity,” she whispered back against his chest.

“I told you, Portia, I need you to believe I’m a man of my word. I needed to fulfill my end of the bargain.”

“I don’t care about the heiress anymore!” Her voice rose, and she hugged him more tightly. “I don’t know why I ever did, but—”

“I know why you cared about the heiress.” He pulled back just far enough to tip her chin up so she met his gaze. “You cared about her because she’ll probably have trouble fitting into this world and you’ve always had trouble fitting into it, too. You cared about her because you care about everyone, even when you don’t show it. I’m just hoping that you care more about me than you’ve been letting on. I didn’t come here to fulfill the bargain we made, I came here because I want a second chance.”

“A second chance at what?”

“I want a second chance to make you fall in love with me.”

This time, she wrenched herself out of his arms with such force, he had no choice but to let her go. “Don’t you get it? I’m already in love with you! Why do you think I couldn’t stay in Utah?” He didn’t answer, so she turned to look at him. A grin split his face. “This isn’t funny!”

“I’m not laughing. I’m happy.” He took several steps toward her, but she held up her hands palm out to stop him.

“I don’t know why you’re happy about it, because I’m sure not. You think you want me now, but how long is that going to last? Forget whether or not I’m in love with you,

I'm not coming back to Colorado with you. I'm not turning my life upside down to be with you only to have you get bored in a few weeks and then decide you'd rather have another no-pressure fling with some Swedish model."

He ignored her outstretched hands and closed in on her. But instead of taking her into his arms again, he stopped a half foot away from her. Still, he had backed her against a wall. She had nowhere to go and nothing to do but hear him out.

"I'm not going to change my mind about this. Don't you get it? I'm all-in. Remember when I said you should never let the person you're negotiating with see how desperate you are? Well, I came here because I'm done pretending I'm not desperate," he said softly. "I can't blame you for not trusting me. I fought this tooth and nail. I did everything I could to keep from falling in love with you." He gestured toward the book where it lay on her coffee table. "Can you blame me? Knowing my family history, can you blame me for being afraid to lose myself in love?"

She shook her head. "No, I can't. But love doesn't have to be like that."

He pulled her roughly back into his arms. "But it feels like that. When we're together, I feel crazy and out of control. I feel jealous and obsessive. And it terrifies me. And the only thing I can hope is that maybe it'll all be okay, because maybe, just maybe you love me back. Maybe I can make you understand you're the most important thing in the world to me. I've screwed up before. You probably don't want to believe that I can do this, that I can be there for you. But I can."

"Cooper—"

"Let me finish, Portia." His voice was forceful and loving and so, so right that it reached deep inside of her. It turned her fears on their heads and shook her resolve.

"I realize this isn't orderly and it doesn't fit into your plan. You can't make a list about this. But I see you, I see the real you and I want you more than I've ever wanted anything in my life. I love you more than I've ever loved anyone."

He paused, took a deep breath. "I know this scares you. It scared me, too. I know you've been hurt before. And maybe it would be easier, safer, if we just walked away from this. But I can't do that. Loving you is the biggest risk I've ever taken in my life, and I know—*I know*—that it's going come with the biggest payoff. If you'll just believe me. If you'll just trust me. If I've learned anything in my life, it's that some things are worth any risk.

"For me, that's you, Portia. You can't be predicted. And I want nothing more than to ride this thing for the rest of our lives. I promise you, if you just trust me, if you just let go, I'll hang on to you with everything I have." He reached up, ran his fingers softly down her cheek. "I'm hanging on to you, Portia. Hang on to me. Please."

Her heart stuttered in her chest. She wanted to believe him so badly that it was an open, aching wound inside of her. She loved him, adored him, wanted him more than she'd ever wanted anything in her life. But could she reach out and take him? Could she do what he said and trust him enough to hang on forever—through the good and the bad, the dangerous and the delightful?

His face moved closer to her, his sapphire eyes bright with hope and love and a need so great it shook her world, turned it upside down. At that moment she was on the edge of a precipice, balanced on the side of a cliff looking down into the yawning emptiness her life would be without him. The same yawning emptiness that had echoed inside her from the moment she walked away from him in Utah.

"Portia—" he started, but this time she was the one who interrupted him.

Lifting one shaky hand to his face, she covered his mouth with her fingers. "I'm scared, Cooper."

"I know, baby. But—"

"Let me finish." She smiled at him. "I've never been a risk taker. I've always played it safe, always done what others expected me to do. But this time, this time I'm going to do what I want. What I need.

"I need you, Cooper. I've always needed you—I just didn't know it. But I do now. And if you want, I'm yours. For now. For tomorrow. Forever."

His face lit up like the sun and he grabbed on to her, pulled her into his arms. And she went, without protest, without struggle, with her heart and her arms open wide. And it felt so good.

If she'd known letting go would be this easy, she would have done it a long, long time ago.

She lifted her face for his kiss and as his lips touched hers, she realized that no, she wouldn't have. Because everything she'd done, everything she'd been through, had been leading her here, to this moment. To Cooper. To the life they would have together. Messy and imperfect though it would be, it was a life she would hang on to with everything she had. Because she was his and he was hers. Forever.

When he lifted his head, he said, "Would you really move to Colorado for me?"

She considered the issue for a moment. "I'm sure not going to ask a snowboarder to move to Houston where it's hot and muggy and never, ever snows. Why? What were you thinking?"

"Actually, I was hoping we might split our time three ways. I need to be in Denver at least half of the time—I can't move Flight+Risk, but I can work remotely a lot. But I wouldn't mind giving Houston a try some of the time. After all, you're the one who keeps telling me I need to be closer to Dalton and Griffin."

She arched up on her toes and kissed him. "Thank you for trying. I would hate it if you let me get in the way of being close to them."

"Yeah. I got that."

"But what's the third place?"

"Bear Creek Lodge. You were right. I got plenty of investors who are interested in funding the resort. Now I just have to decide how to parlay that into something we both can live with. You're right about that, too. I don't want the place overrun by a bunch of trust fund brats."

"You do realize I'm a trust fund brat, right?"

He ignored her jab. "I need you to help me find a happy medium. Someplace you and I can both be comfortable. The way I see it, you and I are both misfits. We need someplace we can both fit in. And maybe someday, if we adopt a bunch of misfit kids, they'll fit in, too. Do you think we can do that?"

He was searching her face, as if he still couldn't believe she loved him. She rose up on her toes and kissed him again. "Yeah. I'm pretty sure I can do that."

After a long minute, he asked, "Is it going to be weird for you?"

"What?"

"Being with me. Since I have the Cain eyes. You're the one who said you'd spent ten years gazing into these eyes." He looked a little sheepish. "I mean, that's got to be weird for you, right? Having me look at you with these same eyes."

She pushed up onto her toes and pressed a long slow kiss to his lips. Then she cupped his cheek and answered him.

"You look at me like I'm the most precious woman in the world. Like you know all of my crazy flaws and love me for them. You look at me with eyes of love. Dalton never looked at me like that."

With those words, he crushed her against him and ground his mouth to hers. A long time later, she pulled away from him and asked, "What would you have done if I'd said it did bother me?"

"I would have bought a lot of sunglasses."

* * * * *

SPECIAL EXCERPT FROM

HARLEQUIN®

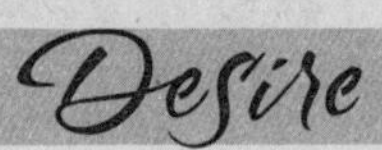

Turn the page for a sneak peek at USA TODAY *bestselling author* Kathie DeNosky*'s*

LURED BY THE RICH RANCHER, the fourth novel in Harlequin Desire's ***DYNASTIES: THE LASSITERS*** *series.*

It's city vs. country when Chance Lassiter meets PR exec Felicity Sinclair….

"Would you like to dance, Ms. Sinclair?"

She glanced at her uncomfortable-looking high heels. "I…hadn't thought I would be dancing."

Laughing, Chance Lassiter bent down to whisper close to her ear. "I'm from the school of stand in one place and sway."

Her delightful laughter caused a warm feeling to spread throughout his chest. "I think that's about all I'll be able to do in these shoes anyway."

When she placed her soft hand in his and stood up to walk out onto the dance floor with him, an electric current shot straight up his arm. He wrapped his arms loosely around her and smiled down at her upturned face.

"Chance, there's something I'd like to discuss with you," she said as they swayed back and forth.

"I'm all ears," he said, grinning.

"I'd like your help with my public relations campaign to improve the Lassiters' image."

"Sure. I'll do whatever I can to help you out," he said, drawing her a little closer. "What did you have in mind?"

HDEXP0614

"You're going to be the family spokesman for the PR campaign that I'm planning," she said, beaming.

Marveling at how beautiful she was, it took a moment for her words to register with him. He stopped swaying and stared down at her in disbelief. "You want me to do what?"

"I'm going to have you appear in all future advertising for Lassiter Media," she said, sounding extremely excited. "You'll be in the national television commercials, as well as..."

Chance silently ran through every cuss word he'd ever heard. He might be a Lassiter, but he wasn't as refined as the rest of the family. Instead of riding a desk in some corporate office, he was on the back of a horse every day herding cattle under the wide Wyoming sky. That was the way he liked it and the way he intended for things to stay. There was no way in hell he was going to be the family spokesman. And the sooner he could find a way to get that across to her, the better.

Don't miss
LURED BY THE RICH RANCHER
by Kathie DeNosky.

Available July 2014,
wherever Harlequin® Desire books are sold.

HDEXP0614